THE MONKEY IN ME
Confusion, Love and Hope under a Chinese Sky

By Caleb Kavon

Proverse Hong Kong

I0635189

THE MONKEY IN ME is a *tour de force* on the fall of the American Empire, the current world economic crisis and the very real crisis of conscience in our culture. It provides a moment of reflection on being human, on our failures, and our ardent desire to find a place of repose on a planet beset by contradictions.

Set in Hong Kong and China, **The Monkey In Me** is decisive, romantic and melancholy, searching for answers. Caleb Kavon challenges our consciences and our lives. He looks forward to the real changes that we all must make in the new millennium.

CALEB KAVON was raised in Hong Kong and the Philippines. A former US army officer deployed in Central and South America, Kavon has lived and worked in China for the past fifteen years. He has travelled the world and remains an avid student of all things. Fluent in Chinese and Spanish, he currently lives in Chengdu China and eagerly awaits the positive changes on our planet which he knows are possible.

THE MONKEY IN ME

Confusion, Love and Hope under a Chinese Sky

Caleb Kavon

Proverse Hong Kong

Caleb Kavon, The Monkey in Me

The Monkey in Me. Confusion, Love and Hope under a Chinese Sky.
By Caleb Kavon.
New ed. pub. in Hong Kong by Proverse Hong Kong, January 2018.
Copyright © Proverse Hong Kong, January 2018.
ISBN: 978-988-8491-31-5

First pub. in pbk Hong Kong by Proverse Hong Kong, 11 March 2009.
Copyright © Proverse Hong Kong 11 March 2009
ISBN 978-988-17724-4-2

Distribution and other enquiries to Proverse Hong Kong,
P.O. Box 259, Tung Chung Post Office,Tung Chung, Lantau Island,
New Territories, Hong Kong SAR.
E-mail: <proverse@netvigator.com>.
Web site: <proversepublishing.com>

Moral Rights: The right of Caleb Kavon
to be identified as the author of this book has been asserted by him
in accordance with the Copyright, Designs and Patents Act 1988.

Page design by Proverse Hong Kong.
Cover design by Agnes Po.

Proverse Hong Kong

British Library Cataloguing in Publication Data (for first edition)

Kavon, Caleb.
The monkey in me : confusion, love and hope under a Chinese sky.
1. Civilization, Modern--21st century--Fiction. 2. Hong Kong (China)--Fiction. 3. China--Fiction.
I. Title
823.9'2-dc22
ISBN-13: 978-988-17724-4-2

Dedication

This book is dedicated to the Chinese People, who have taught me so much and given me such kindness from my youth to the present day. They have made my life very special and I can never thank them enough for each hour, each minute that I have been blessed to spend in their presence.

Caleb Kavon, The Monkey in Me

My Summer Solstice 2008

Oh God, he missed her. It was morning in the desert. The Monkey could see that.

Earlier in the day he had watched some young guy interview The Bone Motley Crue, the hard-rock band.

It was more than he could stand.

The gentry were having a heart-to-heart. Smiling and Serious chat about the number of fans out for the tour.

Hard Rock meets Hard Schmooze. Status Quo begets Status Quo.

Same old drab experts .

Same old me this, me that.

Oh, he was great. Oh, we are going to miss him.

Oh, watch again tomorrow—more of the same droll lost dribble that was made to somehow present itself as news.

The Interviewer was playing Air Guitar and playing the drums.

He just snapped.

There were food riots going on. People could not buy food. Lines were forming in front of the Banks. This was no rising middle class. It was a falling lower class. We no longer had time to do anything but please ourselves.

A world of suffering everywhere .

Petrol was up three hundred percent.

Storms, Earthquakes and Floods and these guys were talking about high school. It was beyond ludicrous. It was verging on insane.

The Fire was just outside our door, and the guyLarry King was playing Air Guitar. Anna Nicole Smith was turning in her grave.

Larry sure had milked that one like a vampire sucks blood.

The situation was that serious. We need to be doing something. Cancel Baseball, Football. Get on this. We needed much more than Al Gore. This was not a case of over-reaction. The World was going to change and soon. We were totally unaware.

Everything we have known and the life we have lived on this planet was going to change. Our Empire was falling. It was a Newnew World. When would we see this?

Air Guitar? The Bone? Motley Crue...

Give me a break. We were in a worldwide emergency. Cancel the Rock tour. Somebody do something. Please.

GM and GE would go bankrupt. Everything we had known was being destroyed in slow motion and replayed.

But it sure seemed that no-one was going to do anything. The Interviewer would make sure of that and The Bone would follow after drinking a pint of Jagermeister on stage and then they would check their stock in Apple. We all would make sure of that. Why do a thing? Let it burn.

This was what our life had become:—Two-week Tsunamis, Two-week Earthquakes and Typhoons. George Clooney on Darfur, and Richard Gere on Tibet.

Close the Border!

Survivor, let'slet's go to an exotic location; learn nothing about the culture or the people and act like total fools. Let'sLet's compete for the win, jumping over logs, making alliances, and talking about ourselves, endlessly. "Let us have our useless fantasy", we all scream.

The daily feed. All total BS.

This was much worse than George Orwell had imagined. Dante was more on target. Things were that bad. The first level of Hell was here. The screams of the starving, angry and confused were deafening.

It was a bath of total idiocy every day.

Go to work, follow your hobby, and then watch American Idol.

Lost. Lost. Lost.

Then again, maybe this is all there was. Meditate or Save Yourself. Get that insurance, pay those credit cards. Was it only him or was this getting beyond belief?

A never-ending barrage of nonsense .

Pushing fifty was a tough one.

How long could one be the fool?

Where was the passion? What was going on in this confused world?

We were in the desert. How we got here no-one knew.

An ancient issue was not being addressed.

It was more confusing every day.

Obviously the world economy was crashing. Ethanol was replacing corn. People were losing their homes. The War in Iraq was dragging on without any direction. We had become an ethnically divided nation joined in some sort of fragmentary culture.

Sure there were good people. But he had met so few. He reviewed everyone he had ever met or lived with. Why was he with these people and not others? What kind of life-track causes this?

Misery by Karma.

He only knew one Saint.

It was an Uncle who had lost everything and everyone in the Holocaust. He never spent money and never argued. He was gentle with everyone. Not one cross word. No bitterness and such suffering.

But so many others.

When you need them, they are not there. When they need you, you'reyou're too busy.

Why the hell was that guy playing Air Guitar?

Wasn'tWasn't the stupidity too obvious? Did it take more to see?

Do we really know why we meet those we are with? Why him and not her? Why here and not there? Who are we?

The TV guy and The Bone had no problems. They knew who they were. They had defined roles. They fit into the tapestry.

What choices decide where we go, what we see, what we do? It was more than some infantile psychology. Or the parents you had. Post-Traumatic Stress. That was his excuse.

All those changes.

What was the purpose?

Another thing he could not understand.

Imprints on our Minds I

An Episode of Cheers.
George Brett and Pine Tar.
Reds and Red Sox.
Jerry Seinfeld—that is New York.
Jimmy Carter was a bad President.
Tim Russert died of a big heart.
It rains in Seattle, and traffic is terrible in Los Angeles.
There are Mexicans everywhere now.
The rose thrown on his Father'sFather's casket. The pauper'spauper's death of his Mother.
The Corvette and the Mustang are great cars.
During the 70s we were down and then Reagan came in and ended the Cold War.
Communism can never work.
The Stock Market will go up forever if you just invest a little at a time.
Whitney Houston had drug problems. But I will always love you.
Cable TV changed our lives for the better.
Macmillan was a failure. The English avoided Vietnam but not Iraq.
Dogs are loyal friends.
Retirement Golf communities and gated roads mean security.
Manhattan is the place to be.
9-11.
Silicon Valley is the center of technological greatness.
Screw Cell Phones.
The 70s Show.
Palestinian Refugees have no right of return, ever.
Clinton and Monica.
Red and Blue States.
Bruce Lee and Tiger Balm Gardens.

Caleb Kavon, The Monkey in Me

Manifest Destiny and the Military Industrial Complex.
We are traditional Allies of the United Kingdom
especially after Thatcher.
The French are Bad. Sarkozy is good.
Russians are backward and Still Bad.
The Great Melting Pot.
The Stress of Divorce.
Titanic, the movie.
Yes, the poor guy is going to sacrifice himself for the
blue-eyed girl.
We know the Titanic Theme Song and All Asians look
alike.
Middle America is where?
 Kobe Bryant can'tcan't win the big one.
We believe in something much higher.
In Iraq, we are fighting Iraqis, Terrorists and Iran as
well as ourselves.

Hong Kong Airport

The Airplane was in its final approach to Hong Kong. The journey of sixteen hours was closing. The rush to bathroom after breakfast, the anticipation of the end was everything. People were only thinking about what they had to do after they arrived. They were already off the plane. Getting ready.

The slow and then sudden movements as the plane hits the clouds and momentarily is engulfed, only to appear again as if nothing happened. The slow turn of the wings as the aircraft approaches, the clunk of landing gear.

The plane made a smooth landing and rolled to the Gate. It was time for him to wake up and put on his shoes. He was back home.

Leaving the plane, he entered the grey white light of the terminal. A terminal he knew so well. The Automatic walkway led straight to Immigration and behind was the Baggage Claim. It was so easy. He had done it so many times. Nothing new here. He missed it all, because he had seen it so many times. But he was not the only one.

The sad truth is: arrivals are for departures and departures are for arrivals.

When the plane arrives we rush like maniacs to depart the airport, to the next place.

When we depart the Airport, we arrive for our flight and our journey and life stops until we arrive to depart.

This was Hong Kong. It was the place where East meets West; the Gateway to China. Hong Kong was a city born of its own frugality and a miracle of life itself. It was efficient and honest and clean and hopeful. The Airport smacked of success with arrogance and the sure confidence of money coming in. More Money, Better Luck.

He grabbed violently at his bag off the carousel and rushed out to start his day and whatever it would bring.

Out in the lobby, he sawLarry King was still playing the Air Guitar again.

Place of Salvation

Like heroic Jerusalem during the Crusades, and the Holy Grail, Hong Kong was his salvation. He owed this place everything. After a cruel and disastrous divorce, he had moved here with his Father and new Step-mother, many years ago.

He owed Hong Kong everything—without exaggeration. Even the graveyards breathed hope. He would never be there without feeling humble and so thankful.

He could kiss the ground and drink the water of the harbour. He felt that strongly.

His greatest regret upon his death would be that he could not be with them here any more. His Heroes and his Greatest Love were the Chinese people. Hong Kong was the Messiah of his life. The most perfect place on Earth. He knew every inch, building and hill-side. He had walked them all.

When he was a child, the then four million inhabitants and their daily struggle, done with the most drastic grace ever, had been his inspiration. Looking out on the harbour, walking every week, travelling in buses, smelling the strange and exotic foods, he was entranced. The shopkeepers and hawkers became his family.

This place had given him hope. Only this place was his home. In his heart, he was from Hong Kong. For here and only here had he ever felt so happy .

But that was another time and another City.

Now he worshipped only the past, and as if in Babylon he was cast out.

But He worshipped it none the less.

Now it was an international city.

Global Banking.

Stock Markets.

15

Caleb Kavon, The Monkey in Me

Hong Kong was the last island of the World System, before the great land mass of Asia and the wild border with China. It was the final frontier of the Empire.

Sometimes he felt Hong Kong now had more tourists than locals. The olden-day kindly Shopkeepers had been exchanged for surly cell-phone shops waiting to pounce.

Tension was now in the air. The golden ring was beginning to look further away. Rising prices, inflation. Worries were in the air. The Olympics were weeks away. Earthquakes, Floods and Typhoons portended problems. Pride was transformed to severe embarrassment. His old love was having problems.

Hong Kong had no sins, nor could it ever be wrong. None of his grave mistakes or foolish decisions had been made there. It was far away. One could think. Sitting on any corner, and watching the world move, was his solace and gift from Hong Kong. . . .

It was the slow careful pace of the elderly, purposeful rush of the successful, hopeless stares of the deprived. And then The Tourists moving—and seeing a place really like no other. Silence was golden, the noise was precious. Hong Kong was precious.

To really see Hong Kong you had to stop. Go in a Noodle Shop and just look out. Watching the city move was the real pleasure. Running from one meeting to another or going to this trade show and that trade show would mean that you missed it all. Stop and look. Its daily motion is the magic. The real heart is there. Take the time. Stop and watch.

This was a vacation. It was his place. He remembered his teacher had cried when Nixon declared an end to Vietnam. He remembered his Father'sFather's joy when he rushed up and told him Nixon was going to China. He remembered the fall of Saigon and the opening of China. He remembered the return to China. He could still see the students reading in the Bus. He could see it all so clearly. As long he as breathed, it would never die. It would be him.

Hong Kong was his heaven.

Thoughts in a Taxi before the Rains: Jet Lag

It really was endless.

This and That.

Endless things and ideas.

My opinion .

Your right to yours .

No wonder everyone was concerned. It was a flood.

But Noah could not float on this stuff. We were full of this concept and that. We had this idea and that. This was right and that was wrong.

The great plan of our civilization .

We can'tcan't all move to the hills and kill our TV. We cannot do much more than try to get some handle on our individual lives and save for retirement and death.

Love?

Yes, maybe that was it. Or was it?

Those loves. Her and Her and Her and Her and Her—and Her—and HER, #7.

Why the Seven Great Loves and Seven Disasters?

Victims and Victimizers.

Why all the changes?

Moving Continents. Forgetting this past for another, later to be also forgotten.

A restless soul.

My claim to fame.

My Story.

He was sick of His Story.

He was sick of the Desert.

Shangri La

One would think Hong Kong was his home forever.

But no, Heaven was denied to him.

He was like an old Satellite forced into another orbit. He was droppedforced into the lobby of a hotel without the grace of floating junks and shouts of muscular fishermen as they lift baskets of fish onto the dock while their children on the boat watch. No Birds were singing and in the distance he could not see the little monkeys moving from tree to tree. The Farmers and the Singing were drowned by some sort of elevator music.

From life into a sterilized world.

Yes, this was a place to avoid the world. Better than Opium and much more delusional.

Shangri La was not some book or place in deepest Asia. It was a hotel. How they ever got the name I am not sure. This was as far from Shangri La as you could get.

Thick carpets and shiny marble .

The clunk of suitcases on the floor during arrivals and check-outs all day long.

False smiles all around.

The credit card approval machine printing the distance .

Newspapers from around the world in the gift shop .

The smell of fresh wax and money .

He went to the Coffee Shop.

A touch of Paris.

Doing deals over the buffet of a hundred items was the main course.

The thinking being, why go suffer in China, when you can buy the same stuff here?

Let us be your representative—don't conduit—don't deal with the mean and dangerous Mainlanders. Deal with us.

This worked for many years, and yes China was not easy. But like the Japanese before them and the Taiwanese, the Chinese were learning, slowly, the same game, and making Hong Kong a peripheral to much of its commerce.

Chinese ports were taking more and more of the Container business and the biggest tourist group was now without doubt the Mainland Chinese, some of whom were on the very first vacation of their lives. Role reversal is not always fun, it stings and burns and every day is just one more reminder.

He hated this atmosphere.

Everyone knowing just what they were doing.

All of his life he had to deal with these ""successful people."". During the 90s it was the Dot-commers. They were making millions and millions on the Dotcom boom. You would hear them in the line counting their stocks as they went up and up. You would see them driving in their new SUVs and the smug looks on the highway. Then all that crashed and the smug looks became blank vacant stares. They had been fooled. Poor fools..

Then in the last decade, the same situation occurred. This time it was investment bankers, and big dealers, with gold watches and Italian suits making deals. The world economy was booming.-"let's—"Let's buy this company in China. The market is growing so fast. We can do the deal. I want fifty thousand of this and that." ."

Everyone was smiling and counting their profits. But Lehmann was gone. There were lines outside the banks. Bear StearnsStearns was dead.

It was almost a pleasure to watch the great Investment Bankers go down howling. How could such smart people fall down so fast? Maybe they were not as smart as they thought. They had screwed up big time. They called it Hubris, but maybe this was just an act of God. How could anyone screw up so badly?

Like Karl Rove and John McCain the reformer, or the Great Change of Obama, they would keep up the spin.

Say this today and do that tomorrow. Have faith in the system, great world masses! It will all work out better in the end. Forgetting that the number of malnourished was growing every day and that tainted milk was killing babies. Our total loss of responsibility was stifling. What was worse, none of us had an idea of what we were doing. We sure acted like we did.

He with the chip on his shoulders; always sure that everyone would be better doing it with him. Like a wounded jackal, unable to close on the prize, he was left to circle at a distance. Surely the bones had some meat?

Ordering Coffee in Mandarin Chinese, to the unhappy non-smile of the English-speaking waiter. Service was getting worse and worse.

The first meeting was with a friend of his now departed Father. He had to meet the great journalist, Arthur Stein. And why on earth he was having this meeting, he didn'tdidn't know. Something for his Father, he guessed.

A Vietnam War Veteran and cigar-smoking crew-cut-wearing cowboy in the 70s and 80s, he was now lost in the wilds of China. Arthur was a pain.

But he was still making an impact, or so he thought.

And of course he really wanted you to know about it. Not speaking Chinese made him doubly effective.

But never mind that, Arthur could recite his long list of accomplishments and make sure that you knew them too. The kind of person who, if you said, ""What a great life you have Arthur;"!" the great journalist would answer with a, "You're"You're jealous. And you should be, Buddy," with a Southern accent and twang.

He never understood that the age of the White Man'sMan's Burden was over and now the poor backward peoples were teaching us a thing or two. He could not see the dark horsemen massing on the plains. They were creating a wave of dust. Thus effectively putting him out to pasture.

But, what the hell, he didn'tdidn't give a damn either. His, "Isn't"Isn't my life interesting"", mass emails were a litany of nothings and so-what's.whats. Not that Arthurhe would ever notice.

His Father had that get-along-with-anyone-", "Hey, let'slet's have a drink!" kind of friendship.

Be part of the team! We are the Experts together.

It didn'tdidn't make his Father any happier. His friends never saw the depression and struggle that we in the family got to know.

Arthur and his Father were made for each other.

Caleb Kavon, The Monkey in Me

Waiting for a Legend
and how wewe got here

He would be waiting a while. Arthur couldn't care less if he was there for a year. He always had to wait for the Great Man. Sitting in some coffee shop, waiting for someone he would rather never see even once for the next thousand years. He could never just say, "no". As a loyal son, he had to wait like a disciple waitingdog for the Master.

Yes, it was tough following the Great Ones. Fifty Years ago, Asia was on its knees—all of it.

Victorious Allies and Starving Koreans, Chinese, Japanese, Filipinos, Malays, Burmese and Indians. . . . They were all starving, and they had nothing.

The last man standing.

Asia was an American lake. There was nothing left in Asia. The War had been terrible beyond words. We were the Saviours.

Must have been tough for the Great Generation.

Living Gods with crew cuts, all products were theirs.

Tough to sell cars and medicine and whatever when you are the only one with anything.

There was really no competition then. Asians did not possess the skills.

For guys like his Dad and Arthur, who left College in the late 50s, the world was theirs. They were here to teach the natives.

Full employment opportunity.

That first house in their 20s.

The Peace Corps and our World to Change.

The clear path to the top.

Essentially they became the bulwark that supported the Vietnam War, our Nation'sNation's first Iraq. Massive buildup of resources supported in full by big business'sbusiness's penetration of new markets.

23

Their parents had suffered in the Great Depression..
They lived the life of kings on the hill.

The Cold War had produced our first conflicts of
the Post Victory World—in Korea and later Vietnam.
China was slowly awakening and changing behind its
Bamboo Curtain.

The main point is, the basis of American dominance
was totally situational. It was not some divine order or
manifest destiny sort of thing. As the last man standing, a
country with great resources, we could not help but
dominate. It was not a Democracy thing, or our God-given
right. It was circumstance bought with the blood of seven
hundred thousand young men and Flashesa Flash of Bright
Light and DeathMisery over Hiroshima and Nagasaki..

It'sIt's not hard to be #1 in a race where you are the
only one with a horse. Good for the ego, but very scary
when everyone else suddenly can ride.

And on this prosperity we lived.

Cheap resources, expanding business and Speed
Racer.

We could not lose.

Then came Vietnam, the Oil Shock.

Nixon and Ford.

We had lost it so quickly never knowing why.

As if our deserved, ""We get everything,"", had
ended. Oh, such a depressing notion. How could it be?

But we got out of it. Reagan came and with him
came, ""Big wins in Grenada and the Fall of the Evil
Empire". Bush Number One following up with Panama and
Iraq. Clinton and Gore saved Bosnia. The World Trade
Center did not fall the first time..

Russia collapsing in front of our eyes and a party on
the Iron Curtain.

The Internet and Stock-market boom.

Roaring 90s.

A Strong Dollar.—Cheap imports from China and
Mexico.

Houses for everyone again.

Credit cards maxed and paid for.

The Ex-Soviet Bloc crying for washing machines and cars. The USSR broken to pieces.

New room for growth.—NATO expanding.

Standing one day in the late, late 90s on the banks of the Rhine River with powerful dollars in his pocket, he had thought: ""I can'tcan't believe it— we really are on top again. What an amazing economy.".".

But like his lies, the lie of the great economy was unraveling. We were a confused race.

Prosperity was built on the backs of endless buying.

An orgy of credit.

Buying ten pairs of shoes every year.

New fashions, new TV, a new car whenever.

Sex in the City. No open sewers.—Should it be pearls or diamonds today? What a lovely wardrobe.

Twenty-five-year-olds in Leased Mercedes.

A huge house out of an old apartment.

All provided by credit and a Bubble.

Our infrastructure crashing.

No new airports, roads. Old bridges. Public transport all out the door.

The Cruise Line vacation, Hey let'slet's go to Spain.

The revenge of Tony Soprano and Hill Street Blues.

Monsters could walk.

We were fools all of us.

The Internet proved not to be the great follow-on money-maker. People became so maxed out on credit that in the end they could not afford the house payment when the variable loan went up. The growth in Eastern Europe went down. The rise of China meant resource price rises. Millions of tons of steel, cement and coal were used like there was no tomorrow. Oil—riding on speculation and a crashing stock market—broke new records every month.

It was the new world disorder.

The poor, who had never left the planet, could never buy. And the poor rich were now not able to keep up the orgy of spending which caused the growth in the first place. Thus the current crash and final reckoning for a system, that only worked for the few, if the many bought in to it. We were stupid and now all would pay. The American Consumer had fallen on his knees.

Our system was built on a US as the Centre of the World model. When the American citizens could not buy endlessly, the system crashed. The Economic model did not account for a hundred million of the new Chinese and Indian Middle-Classes buying cars and using air-conditioning and steel in their houses. The poor in Latin America and Africa never counted for anything.

This was not to mention doing deals with money that never existed. Great economic crimes that would never be punished because we let them all go free. Since no-one could figure out that we owed more than all the money in the world, we just let it happen. These were illegal profits. No bail-out would bring it back. No-one had the cash to buy anything any more.

In the previous twenty-five years our Government collapsed. We forgot the poor, the development of infrastructure and made no other more brave decision than to lower the tax on the rich. We became cripples with buffet appetites and absolutely no sense of proportion.

The World was booming, we were told. Look at India and the Stock Market in Manila. What we missed was that this was just a further concentration of wealth with a very limited spread of wealth. While the numbers looked impressive, on the whole people were still getting poorer and the rich getting richer. We owed more money than all the money in the world. That is what happened, no way of escaping it.

Why communicate when nothing was changing? Why make changes when trillions were spent on new military equipment, to fight any war we managed to create?

Each time a jet fighter took off or a bullet and missile were fired, we had to pay for it. But we were asleep, drunk off our ass, and not watching this. We were dreaming of our new car or our new shoes, and watching TV.

Survivor was on tonight. The Apprentice would be after that. And Brett Farve was a great guy from Mississippi.

Our very humanity was crushed by our need for material satisfaction, we could not stop ourselves. Our only concept of change is and was taking care of Number One.—Ourselves.

Yet dutifully we had Tim Russert and Wolfe Blitzer to explain the world to us. We became fools following a small club of fools. The same fools who taught us to think only of ourselves—could only ever think of themselves. They all sounded so reassuring. Things were booming. They had such interesting lives, and we could all Be Like Mike.

The Straw that broke our backs was 9-11. How could anyone be so bold as to attack us?

It was impossible to contemplate.

How could we be attacked?

And by a handful of terrible young men!

Our response was as predictable as it was misguided.

Like Drunken Sailors, abusive fathers, and confused children, we lashed out. We crossed the World in a fury seeking revenge against dead men. Our bombs and missiles and soldiers went where we should never have gone. We would be fighting terrorists with a blunt hand and an open wallet. We never realized that something must be very wrong in a world where there are weekly suicide bombers. But we would get even. So help us God.

Revenge would be served warm. It would make our enemies stronger, our nation weaker and create an inevitable downfall. Three thousand dead becomes one hundred thousand in a flick of an eye. The Great Power humbled and lost in thirty minutes on a nice September day.

To top that off. . . .

Iraq.

It was not enough to rage. We had to go for more. Holding someone'ssomeone's strategic vision cloudily in our hands—another country was to fall. Enter the loss of more lives, a futile struggle. We would lose Iraq. We would withdraw. They would hate us. They would keep killing each other after we were gone.

Great Job by Dick Cheney and the lost one in the Oval Office.

We should never have been there. They really love us. —We are bringing democracy. The huddled masses cry out for us and more Rock Music from The Bone.Motley Crue.

Be like us, we are the experts. Understand us, we cannot understand you.

Vietnam again and again and again.

More enemies.

Yes, we do not care. Yes, we get off lightly all the time.

Criticize China for one hundred deaths in Tibet and unleash a near-daily car bombing, religious strife and endless war. We should fix our house first before fixing something or someone else. Criticize them for that? But we never face up to our own faults!

We have fought the British, Germans, Japanese, Russians, Italians, Chinese, Vietnamese, Pakistanis, Koreans, Grenadians, Panamenos, Dominicans, Cubans, Nicaraguans, El Salvadorans, Somalis, Libyans, Colombians, Iraqis, Iranians, Afghans, our own American Indians, Filipinos, Palestinians, and the Barbary Pirates.

Who was next?

It never ends.

Interventions, occupations .

We have fought everybody. Then we wonder why the land of plenty is stressed out.

Amazing thing that we cannot stop and think what we are doing.

Amazing thing that we do not cry out, "STOP!"

Wave that Flag, "Country First!"

We are always right.

It is only Pride and it is our Greatest Sin.

Amazing thing that they lie us into this and that. And we never notice a thing.

The cell-phone breaks the quiet of his anger. . . . It is HER, #7.

Love??

Always and again, like Like a Dog looking for approval, he quickly answers. She never does. Like the fool that he is, he expects love and affection that she never gives. He is the last on her mind. She only wants his money. Where is he? Did he send the money to her? He will call later.

Another failure.

Another one who will never really care .

Good Looking Neophyte. Good in Bed. You mess my head.

He is always in this position. Helping and Getting Nothing. Looking for love and getting nothing in return.

They need Us—us,We are the Experts

A sip of this six-dollar coffee and a look at the lobby .

Arthur was bounding in.

It is the confidence that you are supposed to present when entering your Shangri La.

The Grand Lobby, expensive lamps, cool clean air.

Of course he is wearing his light blue safari suit. Pen in the left pocket.

Still in shape for seventy years old. Completely Bald and Completely Cocky.

Still arrogant and so sure of himself.

This is all about him. Oblivious to all around him except for the occasional young Chinese or Japanese Hotel ""friend"".—He was meant for this Hotel and all it represents.

""Hey, Bobby. What'sWhat's going on?"

"Just here waiting for you as usual.—how'sHow's your Stock Market doing?"

"Always a smart ass, I remember you when you were nine."

"And you were thirty-five.".".

A pause...

""So you just got back from Dalian, Arthur? How was it? Northern China is different."

"Not good. I just lost my consulting position in that damn teaching job at the University. You know the Chinese. They will never understand a free press. Just not a place for me. I am a Southerner not a Yankee."

Arthur was always losing one job after another, and he never tried to analyze why. It was always a problem with the Chinese.

""Well, some think CNN distorts the news as much as they do."

"They need a free press, to change."

"They have changed, Arthur, more than any country on Earth. Never has a country advanced more in such a short time. Think about China twenty years ago. So much change it'sit's just hard to comprehend. Thirty years ago, that was one China. Now it'sit's another."

"Not changing fast enough. They need to begin to democratize the society, and the press."

"Arthur, how much more do you want? The US is the US, China is China. We cannot expect them to be the mirror image of us. Is that what you want? A world with Denny'sDenny's and McDonaldsMcDonald's at every corner. ArthurRichard, if you spoke Chinese you might understand them better. You only speak to English-Speaking Chinese. The Bosses and Leaders and Common people don'tdon't speak English. Do you really care about them? You were saying the same things when we lived in TimorPhilippines and in Brunei.Bangladesh. What do you want?"

"No. Of course not, not sure what I want. But forget about it! How is your business? Still not making money?"

He knew this was coming.

"Well, to tell the truth, it could be better. Lots of competition.""

A moment of break from the embarrassment that was coming as the non-smiling waiter, George (he could read his name card now), came and asked Arthur what he wanted to drink.

""Perrier with a slice of lemon.""

This, spoken from a guy who was bornused to live in Mississippi!

""No, Arthur, business is not good. I never seem to get the lucky break."

"Well, you could always work at McDonaldsMcDonald's."

"Yes, maybe I should."

"You know your Father retired at 35thirty-five, Bobby."

"Yes, I know. But that was a different time."

"Yes, he was quite a successful businessman."

"What's going on in Timor?" Bangladesh?

"Well, you know I am quite tight with RamiMujib Khan there. Not good there either. The present government is putting all the Politicians in jail. Not sure what will happen. It keeps dragging on. You know I was there during the War of Independence and last year was honoured at the Anniversary Celebration."

"Yes, I know, Arthur. Best Regards to Rami.—He was a good friend of my Father's."

"Yes, I am a bit upset about the economy. My son told me to buy some stocks last year and they are all tanking. Not good."

"Sell Now! The DOW will go to ten thousand, maybe nine thousand—it could go to eight thousand. Heck, why stop there?—Seven thousand—five thousand—looks possible. I told you last year what was going to happen. The US Dollar is crashing. Run for the hills!"

"Never. It can never go so low. You always only see the dark side. Things will be looking up, after the election."

"Arthur, when we talked about this last year, you told me I was crazy. You don'tdon't sound so sure any more. Can'tCan't you see that this has been a long time coming? We fooled ourselves into being fooled. Now you think the election will solve everything? What election, Arthur? Whoever wins, loses. This is going to be the worst most painful four years we can remember. I think we are going down hard. If the Democrats win, they are finished. If the Republicans win, it's time for chaos. We could go fascist. That is, if we are not going there already. Can'tCan't you see the anger?"?"

Arthur frowned, as if taking it all in.

""Yes. Sure.—And you probably think Global Warming is causing it."

"Not sure about everything. But if the waters rise, this place will be under water. What would we do without Hong Kong? Not to mention, Bangladesh would be under water. Who knows? Anyway your son was right when he quit from the Wall Street Bankbrokerage and retired."

"Damn Right. Something you will never get to do."

"Not looking good for me on that count.".."

Arthur drank his Perrier as if in deep thought. And then drank again.

""I have a date with the MacauJapanese Girl from the ConradFurama Hotel tonight. Might get serious. I will let you know if I hear anything. Tomorrow I have to go to HainanGuangzhou to see about a new position. They need an Expert."

"Good Luck. I hope you learn Chinese one of these years."

"Good   Luck,   Bobby!   Remember McDonalds'McDonald's is always hiring."

"Thanks!—I know. Keep in touch.".."

With that Arthur bounded up and out of there. Their conversations were always like this. No, they were not really friends. Lord knows why he saw him at all. McDonald's always came up and how could we forget his son the Millionaire? He was just another person he would never know..

How could he ever forget?

No, he was not as successful as his Father, either. And yes, in business he was never that good.

Really a failure.

Just breaking even, paying people late   .

Screwing up orders right and left.

Impatient with his suppliers and workers.

He was always losing customers.

Lucky to have even one .

Bad at the accounting .

Never hitting his stride .

Looking across the room at the other successful business persons, he could only wonder what they had. Having your own business was hard. How long would this last or how long would he last?

Of course, he had lost his partner, a kind and decent man, also an old friend, in a fit of stupidity. Now things were tougher—harder to make money. He still believed in his business model and remained hopeful, but a nagging feeling remained always at his side like a leering ghost.

He was going to fail and soon.

Then again, maybe not.

Going up to his room, riding the carpeted, bell-ringing elevator with lighted orange buttons, the leering Ghost was at his side. He forgot about Arthur. He had bigger problems.

Entering the room, he first opened the in-room safe to put away his wallet. Why, he did not know.

Back to the TV .

Weather report .

A typhoon was coming. Of course they had predicted this one completely wrong.

 Like they usually did .

The Typhoon Feng GangShen was first reported to be heading out to sea away from the Philippines.

That was wrong, as it then approached the Philippines. But then it was going to skirt the Philippines and head to Taiwan.

That was also wrong, as it then turned straight into the country, killing several thousands.

Then it was going to weaken and run up the Taiwan Straight.

Wrong again, it was now rushing straight to Hong Kong.

He looked out of the small window. The clouds were rushing in and the wind was blowing plastic bags into the air. Like departing souls, the bags rose over the nearby buildings and out of sight. This was looking like a big Typhoon now.

But the weather person, Monica,Jenny couldn't care less.

Wimbledon was starting and the Tennis would be wonderful. The Typhoon that killed so many in Myanmar was over—news-wise. The key reporter was in Kandahar now. The Earthquake in China was also not news. The two million starving in Myanmar and five million homeless in Sichuan were not issues any more. No-one would cover that.

Dead in the Philippines.—Give *that*, thirty seconds.

The social situation in Pakistan, let'slet's not go there. Too dangerous, we need to report from the hotel.

No need to understand why.

There is a huge Marxist Revolutionary Group in Northern India. Don'tDon't report that.

Tsunamis and Earthquakes that many countries were still recovering from, done that already.

Done that already.

And . . . Done that already.

We would not hear about them for months if ever. . . . It was over. On to something else right away.

Wimbledon would be glorious.

Time to check the market and which bank is going down next. No-one could buy anything if no-one has money.   Simple.

So they got this Typhoon all wrong and some people would die.

Tennis had Roger Federer.

More Air Guitar .

The phone again .

Maybe he should not answer. But, what the hell?

Eric, his pissed-off customer, was looking to see him later. When would he be there?

""I will be there about 5pm. OK?"

Caleb Kavon, The Monkey in Me

Of course it was not OK, like asking your parents what time you wanted to be punished. It was not going to be nice.   How much would it cost?

Still a couple of hours.

Imprints on our Minds II

Suicide, Yukio Mishima and Finland at night.
Total Recall.
Somali Pirates and the Electoral College.
The Partridge and Other Families on TV.
Tom Petty.
The Talking Heads.
Prison Break—Break your IQ with Tony Blair.
Guns and Roses.
Pattern Baldness and Late Night Insurance for
Funerals.
Johnny Cash and Elvis.
Boyz in the Hood.
Homes in Malibu on Fire?
Man U sponsored by AIG.
Arsenal sponsored by Emirates.
Man City owned by an Emir.
San Diego Padres.
Homeless Communities, Hoovervilles or Bushvilles?
Saturday Night Fights.
Why I left her.
Why she left me.
The Cold of Winter.
The Warmth of the Cold War.
Sarkozy. The and the Vichy.
Samurais and Fukuda or is it Abe today? Who
knows? Berlusconi?
No Rest for the Weary and Phantoms over the Trail.
Adidas and Puma.
Betty La Fea—Ugly Betty and Betty White and Little
House on the Prairie.
Rainforests and Immigration and a new set of Tires
and an Oil Change, Please.

Tsim Tsa Tsui

After a short nap to forget everything and jet lag, he set out for a brief walk. It was thirty centigrade. He started to sweat in two minutes. It is always so hot and muggy the day before a Typhoon hits.

Afternoon in Tsim Tsa Tsui, one of the main commercial areas in Hong Kong, was frantic. You need to walk with a certain style with your head down to avoid stepping on someone. You had to move with the speed of the crowd.

Stores everywhere. Indian tailors, ""Sir, would you like a Suit.""?"

Music blaring from the stores selling Cell-phones and Video Cameras.

The cool blast of air-conditioning as it leaked out into the street.

Nike, Adidas. Watch stores, and McDonald's, and Starbucks.

Yes, maybe he should stop in and apply. Maybe he could handle that job.

Stores selling gold, shirts and shoes.

The tourist disaster or heaven .

The Geography was imprinted in his mind. Nathan Road is the big commercial road. The shopping area runs from Tsim Tsa Tsui to Yau Ma Tei to Mong Kok. In the old days, Mong Kok was no-go territory, home to Triads and rarely a foreigner was seen. Now there was an endless procession of foreigners up and down the street till about 10pm when they retreated back to their hotels or out for a party.

The biggest mistake was to take this as China. It was not. It was an island in the Chinese Sea. Like Shanghai and Beijing this was a door, the door the Chinese had created so the foreigners could see what they wanted to see. The gleaming buildings all came from being the door. All business with China had started via Hong Kong. They were the only gate. They got rich by keeping this gate open.

Hong Kong was about success, and flash with it. The number of Mercedes—and nice ones—on the street was amazing. When they had it, they liked to show it off.

But what we never have seen was the satellite neighbourhoods of the public estates. They are the Soviet-style huge buildings that sometimes you can see in the distance, in the places where the tourists never go and are not in the brochures.

Forty stories high with twenty apartments on each floor, they were where so many in Hong Kong lived because of the low rents. These were not communities. Neighbours did not talk to neighbours. Suicides were common and the daily commute from one area to another was both long and hard and expensive. This was not the Harbour Area of his Shangri La Hotel. It was just ninety percent of Hong Kong.

But why worry about this or them or their lives when cheap and beautiful video-phones could be bought in the tourist area? Funny, how we see what we want to see.

When we travel do we ever stop and think about the life of the Hotel doorman or the guy delivering packages on the street? We don'tdon't even give them a look. Some things never change. As you check in, do we ask them how long they commuted in the morning, and how much it cost? They are tired and working the best they can to take care of their families. Get to know them before you get to know the place. They are the heart of any place and your first door to reality.

He knew these streets well. There he had bought his watch. In another place, the Sony Notebook that had died in three months. There, a cell-phone or five. Shoes, over there.—Here they had his size.

A necklace over there for HER—#6—was bought at one of the dozen jewellery stores.

39

Caleb Kavon, The Monkey in Me

And down the Street was Swindon'sSwindon's—where he bought his books. It was really his Father'sFather's bookstore. But in the spirit of keeping the tradition, he always bought his books there. This was one great bookstore that brought the world to the Expatriates, and good reading and books to travelers in need of information. It was Hong Kong'sKong's oldest English bookstore in the same location for more than forty years.

He stopped at a news-stand to get some cigarettes and took a moment to look at the gossip magazines. In happier times Hong Kong was a rumour mill, with lots of Star- worship in a very small-town way.

Last year the big case was about one of the stars, Edison Chen, who allegedly liked to take pictures of his multiple sexual conquests. The pictures were, of course, sent all over the internet.

Some of the pictures were of the woman considered the most beautiful in Hong Kong and a great actress, Cecilia Cheung. She had separated and might divorce because of the mess and had disappeared.

He was still in love with her anyway. His secret dream was to marry her one day. But there were no pictures today, so he had to suffer another lifetime without her.

Cecilia, where are you? Yes, this was not very faithful, but he loved Cecilia no matter what. Really that was his dream girl. He couldn't care less about the pictures. She was perfect. It was a real romantic crush and he could not get over it. Number Seven was in trouble. Cecilia was the be-all and end-all. He would leave them all for Cecilia, if only he had the chance.

He checked his watch.

He had just enough time to stop in the cell-phone shop. Though he had shopped there many times in the past ten years, each time was like the first time. They did not know him this time any more than the last time.

""How much is that one?"?" he said, pointing to the Nokia model She—#7—had ordered him to buy. His

40

mistake was, he said it in Mandarin Chinese, .and the people in Hong Kong could speak Cantonese and some English but very little Mandarin. For some this was almost an insult; a foreigner speaking better Chinese than them. This time the sales guy was not mad, but thought it was funny.

"One thousand five hundred Hong Kong Dollar.""

No plural in Chinese for money, no plural. . . .

In the back of the narrow store full of cell-phones, digital-cameras, MP3s and Notebooks, the other sales people were arguing with a Mainlander who had bought a bad notebook some weeks ago. Of course they would not give him his money back, which is what he wanted. It was getting heated too. Some nasty names in Mandarin were beginning to fly.

Despite the fact that, for the last decade, more and more Mainlanders have been coming to Hong Kong for visits, no-one is completely comfortable. Hong Kong business people who had daily dealings with the Mainland Chinese were a bit intimidated by China'sChina's rising power. The Chinese RMB had revalued so that it was now twenty percent higher than the year before. The HK Dollar which was pegged to the US Dollar had fallen. Chinese buying-power was up. Hong Kong was part of China. Hong Kong was now China and everyone knew it.

Time to Learn Mandarin.

So there was tension. China was growing by leaps and bounds. Hong Kong was becoming just another of the cities in China. Mainlanders were really calling the shots; and Hong Kong was listening in full.

Every day over two hundred mainland Chinese cross the border to settle in Hong Kong. Over time, the population of native-born residents was dropping and Mainland-born residents was growing. Over the next fifty years, the demographics would change completely.

But this of course was a real perception thing. Most of the Hong Kong population was from China and arrived just after the Revolution, mostly from nearby Guangdong Province, but also from Shanghai, Shantou and Fujian. So this was really the Second mass immigration, only much slower.

Much of the problem was from the past. China of before was bad and a new life had been made in Hong Kong. Now the same forces their parents had fled were back. There was an ingrained fear of the Mainland that would take time to alter. The new immigrants were wealthy, not the type of immigrant leaving everything behind. They were specially sent with a project of slow but sure domination. This was impossible to miss as they ever so quietly became the majority in some districts like North Point and Causeway Bay. The changes were soft and almost imperceptible, but people in Hong Kong could sure feel it.

On the outside, you would not notice any changes. This was a handover successful beyond all expectations. China had done a great job. The main issues were always going to be economic. As in all places, if everyone was doing well you would not hear much complaining. But things were changing.

The Chief Executive lived in the Colonial Governor'sGovernor's previous Mansion. It was said he had ruined the Feng Shui of the mansion because he was obsessed with seeing all the Chinese Mainland TV Stations and had put a plethora of Satellite-dishes in the wrong place.

It could be true. He started off really well and now there were lines of people outside the Bank of East Asia withdrawing their hard-earned money. And it was true, he was a little too eager to please China. But what could he do? He was just a puppet manager. There was no escape and there would be no democracy during his life time. China was the Boss.

Don'tDon't mess with Feng Shui.

The argument in the store had just died down as the Mainland customer decided to buy even more. He looked away and back at the salesman.

""One thousand three hundred Hong Kong Dollar, I buy" ."

A small and insignificant frown. ""OK,"" said the salesman. And the phone was his.

It is often said that the Freedoms in Hong Kong are a test case for future democracy in China. The answer is yes and no. Though Hong Kong does have assembly elections for one portion of the Legislative Council, the real power lies in other hands. Business communities—be they transport or technology or anything else—hold seats and really just rubber-stamp the Chief Executive of Hong Kong'sKong's Special Administrative Region. Most importantly the Chief Executive must be approved first by China.

This is far from a Democracy. With a Pro China party holding a large number of the seats, and the business community making the decisions in back rooms, it was a one-way street to Chinese Control.

In fact, it is a functioning representation of reality in Hong Kong. Business calls the shots with Chinese Government design and approval. And do not cross the line. A leading Democratic politician had recently been severely beaten in broad daylight in a local McDonald's.

McDonald's again!—That Arthur was really getting to him today.real jerk.

But in Hong Kong it is managed really quite well. Law and Order, Rule of Law, and a sense of purpose have all been maintained. This is a credit to all of Hong Kong and should be well remembered in future Chinese History. Good management is good management. Hong Kong is and will remain the best-managed city in China.

From a barren island to a great city.

He took a short walk back to his hotel to get ready for the punishment.

Imprints on our Minds III

John Travolta—just light up that Air Liner and park it
at home, that is so cool!
Letterman in Afghanistan.
Global Warming.
My Parent'sParents' Wedding.
Curse or Blessing?
Do it yourself at Home Depot.
Trips to Hong Kong.
Love and Hate.
Energy Crisis #1.
Ethiopia invades Somalia. The Rape of Nanjing.
Famine breaks out in Ethiopia.
Bengalis in Haiti on Peace-Keeping Missions.
 AROD.
Mini-Skirts and flip-flops.
Energy Crisis #2.
This is not an Energy Crisis.
The fundamentals of the economy are sound.
Colonel Sanders in Ecuador and the Kandahar
Restaurant in the Taj Mahal Hotel.
Bee Gees on late night Call-in Radio.
The Peak in the Smog and Children with Asthma.
Prince and Rush Limbaugh.
Long Trips to Lai Chi Kok Amusement Park.
Paris is beautiful just don'tdon't park your car in the
suburbs.
Fox and Fox and Fox and Fox and Fox and Fox and
Fox *ad infinitum/ ad nauseam*.
On Ramps.
The price of Bread.
Halloween Traffic.
Please no more Superman Movies and Spiderman
Movies.

Pirate Movies are out too. Batman? Please retire him, it's just not real.

This is now a Real Crisis.

Hillary voters.—It'sIt's not about Race at all. There is no Race Card.

Secretary of State???

The EU has created large Polish communities in Scotland.

McCain after Prison and then what? How many homes does he own?

The View for all its worth.

We don'tdon't see America, the way you see America.

Wan Chai

Instead of taking a cab to his funeral with his customer, he decided to take the Star Ferry. Before tunnels and bridges, this venerable transport system had been the main link between the mainland and the island of Hong Kong. In the old days it took over ten minutes. Now it was down to seven minutes as a result of land reclamation that had occurred all over Hong Kong.

He was still hoping to see Cecilia.

Where the world'sworld's vessels once moored in the wide harbour, it was now just a choppy river. Instead of looking at the serenity of the Peak of Hong Kong Island he looked at massive skyscrapers, HSBC, Bank of China and AIG. They say sunset is the best time to go. I guess the sunset will overcome the new global order? Maybe they are right. It is beautiful.

It was a good break before the bag-pipes began to play at his wake with Eric.

But then he got lost. The old, venerable, and ever so familiar Ferry pier on Hong Kong Island had recently been changed and it was his first time in the new "Terminal." Instead of walking out to a sea breeze and waiting taxis in front of an idyllic green park, he followed the crowds through an overpass and found himself in a shopping mall looking at empty stores selling Prada and Versace and only God knew what other expensive brands, some he had never even heard of. He could hear no Chinese spoken, only English, as the Bankers went home for the day. He deduced that the Market must have fallen again by the sighs and long faces he saw as the men in black suits and office-workers passed with stunned looks. Their walked like robots unhappily; not one smile could be seen. It was like a nightmare. It was not like his idea of Hong Kong at all.

He could not figure out where to go, and walked in a maze like a rat for fifteen minutes, through the Mall and into a hotel. Like a lost late puppy he had to ask the Indian doorman where he could get a taxi. He had lost twenty minutes and was totally disorientated by the ordeal. Why did they move the Ferry? It must have been so you could get to the Mall. Misery in its most elegant form is often disguised.

After a ten-minute cab ride he was at a restaurant waiting for his customer in some totally unauthentic Australian-themed restaurant. It was so appropriate to be seated near a boomerang because that was why he was here.

Boomerang.

Back to you.

This was not going to be fun. Several containers of keyboards were being returned. The Chinese factory would not do anything nor could they return them to China. This happened at least once a year. Although he did Quality Control onQC the units, there was always one big problem coming. It was impossible to explain or excuse.

Working with Chinese Factories was always tough. You could do ten shipments all with no problems and then number eleven was bad. It could be a malfunctioning IC, or a bad mould. Anything could happen. Products could work when you tested them and the IC could fail after a short period of use.

That seemed to be the case here. Though some of the products were fine, the failure rate was unacceptably high. Eric wanted to return all of them; and he had a point. The problem was that the Chinese would swap only the bad ones, and then again maybe not. You never knew.

The Keyboard factory could be bankrupt when he got back to China in several days. If they were there, it would be a tough one to get out of.

Wan Chai, Oh Wan Chai!

Home of uncountable hangovers .

Suzie Wong was gone. But the very ground held generations of memories:—of sailors looking for love, drunken nights, Strip-clubs, bars and restaurants. It was a night place. For the foreigners of old, a trip to Hong Kong meant a trip to Wan Chai. Though some new bar areas have opened, this remained Ground Zero.

In fact, Hong Kong and much of Asia undergoes a complete transformation during the night. What appears ugly in the day is magical when one million bright lights come on. On the buildings, in the restaurants, the world is lit in Neon and LEDs. For some reason your energy goes up, life seems more special and the night is on.

People change too. The Business people head for the fancy dinners. The workers make the long bus trip home. Pretty girls suddenly begin to appear as if they had just woken up, which in fact they have. The Clubs stay open almost all night. It is just fine to go out and party at 12 midnight. You will not miss anything. Two in the morning, what is that?

There are two worlds, night and day. Two systems.
Law and Triads.

The Triads run most of the entertainment venues, and other businesses must pay protection-money. This, like so much in Hong Kong, is done in an extremely civilized way. Though there are occasional flare-ups of violence, they are rare.

It would be almost invisible to the naked eye. The two worlds merge seamlessly, as they are part of the same superb system.

As a foreigner, you would miss this entirely and it would be rare for a Chinese to confide the details of the system. But it follows a clear and logical path and does not damage or interfere with the assumed success of the city.

People like to bet on horses and soccer, and to have sex with young beautiful girls, and the Triad provides these services, which a Government cannot. There is a very sane unspoken coexistence between the two. Logic does prevail.

Eric Johnson Parker, his customer, would be oblivious to all of this. Not speaking Chinese, Not drinking,

Not messing around, and always Hating the Chinese. He would never go native. Six foot three, all-American, with Golf Shirt and Chinos, a big Rolex on his wrist and a Beer Belly, Eric was obviously very angry. Bobby had always thought Eric would have been happier with another life. Not one smile ever crossed his lips. It was never going to be more than just business. If ever there was a candidate for suicide, it was this guy. He was what we had all become. Scowling, knowing everything, tolerated. He would always be just The American Tourist, The American Businessman, The American Government.

Facebook and My Space. He was there.

My. My. My.

Misunderstood. Miserable .

""So there you are, Bobby! I thought you might not show up."

"I wouldn'twouldn't miss this for the world! Sorry you are having problems with those keyboards. Hope I can help solve it for you."

"Yeah, right! That'sThat's what they always say. You are really becoming a Chinese now. Aren'tAren't you?"

"Not really, Eric. I was a US Army Officer in Combat did you forget?"

"Yes, but that was then, now you are just like them, always messing up."

"Eric, you have bought three hundred containers from me. The problems have been few and far between. Let'sLet's work on fixing this."

"OK, Bobby, what are you going to do?"?"

The Waiter showed up, never-smiling, and asked themus what they wanted to drink.

""Diet Coke, for me,"," said Eric.

""Red Bull Vodka. Make that a double,"!"

""Right away, Sir,"," chimed the Waiter, Sigmund Lam, by his name card.

Eric smiled.

""Starting early today?"

"Yes, Eric. I had a long flight. I just arrived this morning. I really hope we can get this solved for you. I would much rather we met under different circumstances, not in this Australian Fake O'Steak place and I just got lost in the Mall by the new Ferry Terminal. What a misery to find a taxi there now."

"Yes, I know. It is harder and harder now. What should we do to solve this?"

"Eric, go ahead and return the containers, I will send you the address next week. Not sure where they are going or what we are going to do. I need to inspect the full lot, find the problems and get back to the factory to see what we can do. You know they don'tdon't care anyway. But I will do my best to get you new products soon."

"OK, get back to me. This really pisses me off. This is happening more and more and I'm not sure why. I have five guys that went bankrupt with my money. It is getting really difficult to trust anyone now. Not even you, Bobby. I am here in this damn place, nowhere to go, trying to manage my life and now this. I really hate this."

" But Eric, you are really successful. Your company kicks butt."

"Not like this, too many problems. Really hate it here and this business is miserable."

"Wow, if you keep talking like that, my next drink will be a triple. Hell, the whole bottle!"

"Yes, you can escape. I don'tdon't drink. I hear in China they call you the Monkey King. They must call you that because you make mistakes like a Monkey."

"Good Joke, Eric. Well, let me know if you want to go out later. You did get drunk that one time in Taiwan."

"No. I need to go swimming."

"OK, Eric, sounds like fun. Call me anyway."

"Lots of Girls there, that'sthat's what you like Bobby, isn'tisn't it?"

"Eric, not sure any more, but yes, going out can be fun. Can'tCan't sit around moping all day. I mean, come on, Eric, have some fun! I have never seen you with a Girl. Is there something I should know?"

"OK, call me later. I'll see.".".

With that he was gone. Wow. With relationships like this who needs anything? I mean, why talk to anyone?

Eric at least had some empathy, but nothing was there. Arthur couldn't care less. Or if he cared, he could not show it. Yes, that about summed it up. What was he doing with all these people? No-one said anything about their feelings and life. This was one of our biggest problems.

Just idle chat. Be strong! Be Tough!

One more wasted interaction. Everyone was playing Air Guitar.

This was just one big make-believe.

What did he expect? Everyone was going to pour their heart out to him? He should have been a shrink instead. This is just how it was. It was always just "like" or "not like". The list of all the people he had never known was amazing. People just wouldn'twouldn't open up to anyone now or ever. It was like his Father told him on his death bed.-"—"Be Tough."!"

Why not open up?

We are only here for a short time. Better to be direct. Give up the barricades. Get to know someone. Be a friend. State your fears out loud. Beg for help and mercy.

What is everyone waiting for? There are no gold medals for life. Breaking out is possible. It was what he dreamed of doing. How could it happen for him and everyone? That was the real issue. What we needed was this opening. This had to be it.

He looked at his phone again. It was HER, #7. The phone name said it all, "PAIN". Her father was sick. Did I send the money? Did I get her phone? She was even more stressed out than before. With a day like this, how could he get anything done? He would do it tomorrow, for sure. Bye-ee.

The Monkey was stressed.

Now it was his turn to escape. Screw it all. He called his old Hong Kong friend, Leon Chan.

""Lets go out and get wild, Leon.""

"Good. See you at 10pm. Wan Chai."

Imprints on our Minds IV

John Glenn orbited the earth and a Monkey beat him to space.
 We nuke the Japanese and now they are part of our Defense Alliance.
U2 is a great band and The Rolling Stones still have it.
Having Affairs is wrong. Men do not have double standards with women.
Universal Justice is when you break a heart and then you get your heart broken.
OJ Simpson and Jimmy Kimmel LIVE. So meaningful.
 New England in the Fall and Wall Street before the Fall.
God Bless America.
Reggie Jackson. George Carlin and Rudy G.
 Vietnam and Grenada .
Spring Break and Cruises.
Rum and Coke.
Cancun is OUR vacation paradise.
American Taliban.—Jail him for life.
Wow, are those Obama fans going to be disappointed!
Tiger Woods at the US Open.—What a display of true courage! How did he hurt his knee?
The Terminator. The Governor.
Rodney King and Riots on the Street.
Go Aggies! Go Hawkeyes! Let'sLet's go, Bucs!
Kosygin, LBJ, Haiphong.
The Fashion Industry. We are obsessed with serious Anorexia. Don't miss the Paris Show!
Eight is not enough and Miracle at Christmas.
 The Cukoos'Cuckoo's Nest and that movie where the guy wants to kill his wife.
 John McCain has a clear idea of who he is.

Caleb Kavon, The Monkey in Me

Bob Dole, American Hero.
 Mrs Dole, Senator.
That makes sense?

Montego Bay

Back to the hotel for a nap and shower. Phones were turned off. The typhoon was bringing big winds now. Despite the incompetence of the meteorologists, typhoons were the ultimate in weather.

An Asian Typhoon.—The Great Air-Cleaner.

Barometric pressure is dropping by the minute. Winds are howling. Rain is fresh from the sea.

It roars. It will have its way, nothing is beholden to it. You could feel them coming. The tropics were having a nightmare.

Still it was a long way off. Another seven hours and it would be here.

Time for some sleep.

He had a dream.

Not a Martin Luther King type dream. The kind we all have.

Things that don'tdon't make sense.

The rambling of our mental consciousness.

It'sIt's not like you wake and say, ""What a great dream." You wake up and say nothing to anyone.

He dreamt he was in a Montego Bay. Sounds like Jamaica. But it wasn't.wasn't. There was a green sea and some small beach on a partially yellow-grey overcast day. He could see some small green islands off old Kung Fu island out in the coast. They were the kind you see in old Kung Fu Movies. small Bay.

Standing next to him were two older men in what we now call Mao suits. He could see the white stubble on their faces, cigarettes in their wrinkled hands. He felt they were not hostile, but also they were not happy and not really paying much attention to him. Behind them was a small thin factory with red Chinese characters painted on the wall. The cement was also yellow-grey.

They told him in Chinese that there was no problem that he was there. He could see a Red flag blowing off to the side.

He thanked them and bowed and then walked over to the very narrow beach. At some point he sat down.. The sun was going down, the clouds turning black. In the distance he saw a huge wave coming. A Tsunami was coming. Not like the South-East Asia one, but pretty big, sucking the water from below.

He knew he had to get out of there. He rushed back, climbing up a rope mesh. Where the factory had been was now a wall. No steps there but some holes in the wall and some black padding on top. He stepped in himself up and was ready to pull himself up when the wall of water came.

He held on for dear life. The water passed, but it felt like the Wind. He fell down on the sand.

Looking back at the ocean, the wave was gone and the sea was normal. He stepped back into the holes in the wall and pulled himself up. Nothing was there. All he could say was, ""Montego Bay.".."

Waking up and turning his phone back on, he thought of HER, #7. Deep in another mood-swing he felt bad for her. Her Father was sick.

Poor Farmer'sFarmer's daughter.

She was stuck with him. Her beauty wasted. Eighteen years younger than he. She was probably bored out of her mind. He was not young any more. Other than being the life of the party when drunk, really nothing special. The old foreigner, who snored, needed to lose some weight, and every day said he loved her. Pathetically clinging, expecting more than could ever be there. She was probably the victim here, not him. Damn. Love. Hate.

He should call her back. But no, the money would come up. Not a conversation. She never asked how he was anyway.

The International News was back in full glory. This time, no Weather Report. Of course the Typhoon was coming here. But the underline scroll was still saying it was three hundred kilometres away.

Robert with the Glasses, or whatever his name was.

The life of the International Business Traveler .

Looking so cool in his London Fog .

He was telling us about some new hotels.

Yes, this was the life that they wanted to paint for us. We, the viewer, were part of this new class. CNN was in every hotel. It was our Pravda. RobertRichard was the Pravda Narrator.

Our booming economy means deluxe vacations and first-class flights to Davos and back. RobertRichard will show us how to do it.

It was irritating him again with his booming god-knows-what English accent. He had moved from the news team and now was doing this embarrassing programme, showing us the sights.

Going to sleep .

Nice shorts, Robert.Richard. I really hope they find all the lost bags at the new Terminal in Heathrow. An Advert for Qatar Airlines was followed by one for Emirates, and some advert about planting trees.

Weren'tWeren't we, the world'sworld's international upper class, just simply wonderful? No messy scenes, no problems for us. We have it made in our five-hundred-dollar-a-night hotels. We can all stay there. Stock Market be damned! We will just bloody ignore it all. Won'tWon't we RobertRichard?

Well, now. Back to the News. Typhoon still off target. Oh, I know.

It'sIt's Mugabe week. No elections. Tsvangirai has just left the country.

Well, we have these sorts of elections in Egypt, Syria, and Kazakhstan. No-one says anything.

What about Uzbekistan, the land where no-one smiles?

Yep. Same thing.

Where is the outrage for these elections? Never hear a word.

Not that Mugabe and his goons are nice guys. They are not. But Zimbabwe does not have oil.

We are all so selective. We are all so wrong.

Russia is bad. Georgia is good. Ukraine is peaceful without Mafia and Thugs. It is a really happy place until it defaults to the IMF like Pakistan.

Go NATO! Save the Free World! (Or was that Afghanistan?)

So, we will just scream bloody murder and stay silent about the plethora of other dictatorships, emirates, kingdoms etcetera, where there is no democracy, but oppression twenty-four hours a day, and armed check-points every ten kilometres.
Never ends and never makes sense.

Let'sLet's just call a cat a cat. Or is the saying, "Do we smell a RAT?"

But we can'tcan't and we never will. I mean, Camp David has some visiting Emir, who, like the Pharaohs, has an army of construction workers/slaves living in squalor behind the sand dunes, while the international types just drive by on the new highway they constructed for nothing. New Orleans is still gutted. But we have the money to drop bombs on Afghan Wedding parties?

Think about it. Nothing makes sense. They say, "Hate Iraq!" We hate Iraq. They say, "Hate Iran!" We hate Iran. They say this and we believe them until next week when we should hate someone else. You would think that the USA, which is made up of people from all countries, could understand them all the better. But no, we can'tcan't understand them at all. Amazing. We have the nicest people in the world with the nastiest most destructive government in history. Amazing.

Bush was begging for lower oil prices, knowing full well things would only get worse. The Stock Market was bouncing its ways down. They were telling us it was just turbulence, but both engines were having trouble and the mountain was in front. Bush was just trying to make through the term without the final disaster. McCain was praying the same thing, and Palin and Obama were locating Turkmenistan on the map for the very first time.

Democracy my butt, Mr President!

Save the Banks! We need to. If they couldn'tcouldn't figure out the disease they caused before it hit, how on earth could they ever find a cure?

Where is Moses when we need him? Let my people go!

We have lost the bubble, as we used to say in the Military when I was young.

Oh then, this news! A Software KingBill Gates is retiring.

Oh my God!god—Please, I beg you.

Let'sLet's have a party. Or an international war crimes tribunal. There should be some charges brought, about selling incredibly over-priced software for over fifteen20 years. Yes, it is the best that there was. But look at the prices! The diskettes were more expensive than oil.

It was so dishonest from start to finish. If it costs X$20 per unit to make something, how can you charge X times $two hundred per unit?? Who was ripping off whom? Modern Robber Baron lays low.

Heck even oil companies don'tdon't gouge like the software king did. But that'sthat's capitalism. If you own the only well of water, make sure the customers pay big time. Immorality at its apogee.

What about a famous Home Page? What rubbish! The main headline today reads ""How to make your Girlfriend Really Jealous" or ""Ten Keyssecrets to Healthy Eating" or ""Best Malls in America"" or ""The Most Beautiful and Ugliest Cars Ever".

ItMSN.com was total trash. It was both useless and ignorant. People are not nearly as stupid as they make us out to be. Everyone has something special to say and think.

We want meaning not content. We want to know each other and break out of this temple of garbage.

Thanks! Bill. You made the world in your own image.

Petty, Grey and Simple was this world. There are no colours in computer code.

I mean, talk about no impact! The Software KingBill was selfish to the core.

There is more to life.-Bill. Enjoy your bunker!

I really do understand why you never graduated from Harvard, or was it MIT.—,The humanity classes would have killed your business "instincts".

Then they tell us he is going to give some huge sum of money to the poor.
Yes I know about the Bill and his Wife charities. Great thing, even Warren Buffet joined in. Is that going to change the world?

Go and do good to salve your conscience.

Go ahead and writeWrite a book on philanthropy, even though you have never left the Country without going to Davos or flying in your big beautiful Corporate Jet.

For the Software King, it's just another business to manage.

Pay the NGO'sNGOs two hundred thousand dollars to go to a country where they can'tcan't even speak the language. It is just something to keep our ""Aid Experts"" busy. Make sure those Indian women never have babies!— Indira Gandhi already tried that.

This was the aid no-one wanted or needed. Pushy, arrogant, and insensitive Aid Experts with khaki-pocketed shorts and expedition backpacks, going to change the world and help the poor ignorant natives. They are worse than our soldiers, who are just following orders and are decent and normal.

To change the world you need to get your hands dirty. Not just write cheques. You need to understand more than the English-speaking élite. Try to really get to know them, then you might have some idea. You cannot learn about a place during a two-year tour. Forget it!

But not the Software King. He knowsBut not Bill Gates and Wife... they know all there is to know.
There will be a very special place in Hell for them.

But really, think about it. Is this the best that our best and brightest have to give?

No concept of real impact.

All that Money in his hands! What a waste!
He Billcould really have done something. But eating smaller companies was more important.

He does not need to put on glasses. He needs a seeing-eye dog or a visit to the nearest Church, Mosque, Synagogue or Temple.

Leave the PalaceBill! Walk on the earth again! Follow in the path of Buddha! You are so far from enlightenment.

Big Waste #2 or maybe #1.

Those rich young guys from a Search Engine.

How without a clue could you be? Let'sLet's go to the moon! Let'sLet's talk intelligent-sounding tech words and do nothing at all for humanity. Let'sLet's fly around in our own love-shack plane!

What?

Is that all there is, Gentlemen?

Four hundred US dollars a share for a Search Engine? What a joke!

Make a copy Cell-phone.

You guys are just a big waste of time in the grand scheme of things.

What about Richard Branson? Just more air without substance. Madonna? Bill Gates? The Google People? Warren Buffet?

Let'sLet's fly London to Bangalore with Champagne and a Stewardess Beauty Contest on Board, while we forget we have Hindus killing Christians and Moslems killing Hindus and a huge Communist rebellion thirty thousand feet below us. Let'sLet's balloon around the world, while not seeing how absolutely meaningless it all is. You are an empty idol who will give us nothing.

Flying across the English Channel in between vacations on our own private island means absolutely nothing.

These Icons of our modern-age Paganism give us nothing. In their world, the absence of and separation from compassion and our very loss of humanity are glorified.

The Tower of Babel was absolutely a silent experience compared to the foolishness that we have unleashed in the past fifty years.

Our new Gods are CEOs, and successful businessmen. We listen to them as if somehow the price of their stock would give us something more than the stupid game it had all become.

Humility is mocked and False Idols are gods.

Man does not live by bread or IRAs alone. Ever heard of that concept?

Anything else but getting market-share means nothing. We have taken what is just not central to life and glorified it.

Love, Family, Compassion, Sharing and Community have been replaced by the group of fools that open the Stock Exchange everyday.

The clapping and pounding of the gavel that we must suffer through every day is our new temple. It is our new temple of fools and lost souls. As if we could take it with us! This emptiness is vaster than Siberia or the oceans of the world or our small universe for that matter.

Making a buck means nothing if a child is starving. Isn'tIsn't that more than obvious?

Screw trips to Mars, when people are malnourished in Cavite Province. If you don'tdon't know where that is, look it up. If you can'tcan't figure that out, you are lost. There are just no excuses any more.

Scream about being kidnapped in Colombia. That is fine. Just remember, poverty is also a kidnapping. A young man or young woman with no future due to poverty is kidnapped and there will be no rescue-mission for them. They are jailed by poverty and watching Kobe Bryant sell sneakers and wear gold. Who is kidnapping whom? What is right or wrong? These are simple questions that no-one wants to ask.

Just don't even try to be surprised when they bomb your hotel or commit acts to kill and terrorize you.

They said the new frontier was Space. But no, the only new frontier left to be opened was the frontier of our hearts.

Always has been and always will be. The world is a mess for this and only this reason.

Too idealistic for you?

No.

One hundred percent correct, all the time, every time.

We never needed, ""the Right Stuff."". We needed to care and turn brutality to softness. We needed to sacrifice ourselves for a higher cause. That was our destiny, not Sushi and Martinis on a Saturday night or being seen in the new club with very interesting people.

We were worshipping a Success that means absolutely nothing, Success that was nothing more than complete failure.

This was the work of a failed generation completely content with themselves.

Failed Humanity in its intolerable vanity. We were in the midst of a hundred years of total failure. Our Great Ones had failed us completely for the past sixty years. We had been completely wrong.

Garbage in, garbage out.

Montego Bay. Sure sounded good to him now.

Thanks to all of them, he was ready to go on a bender.

Party Time

This was the highlight of so many on their trips to Hong Kong. Don'tDon't let anyone fool you. When they come back from Asia with the coy and knowing smile on their faces, you know the story.

Thousands of Guilt-ridden husbands and fathers who become less and less Guilt-ridden.

It was a Man Thing. Hypocrisy and lack of feeling.

It'sIt's like Bored House-Husbands, or Sex in the City.

It is the real McCoy. Hong Kong has a huge divorce rate among foreigners because the pressure is too much to handle. Coming from morally more strict societies, people go crazy. The Chinese handle it in their stride because, well, it'sit's always there. Not the rest of us.

Of his customers, probably twenty percent did not go out and look for women. That left eighty percent ready to go.

And he was their willing guide to Hell.

Leon Chan, his good friend, was waiting for him at one of the bars on a side street. Leon was all that was good and decent about Hong Kong. They were roughly contemporaries, though with different lives. Leon'sLeon's mother had worked eighteen hours a day in a toyplastic flower factory. Leon'sLeon's Father was a bustaxi-driver. Both parents sacrificed everyday for years to put Leon through school and on his way to a better life.

His parents and the whole generation with them were Saints. Hard-Working and decent, doing everything they could do to make a better world for the first thing on their minds, their children. They were like His own Grandparents in the US. Leon'sLeon's parents built Hong Kong. When you see the glistening sky-scrapers and the very modern city that Hong Kong is, know that it was built by Leon'sLeon's parents and you owe everything to them.

Caleb Kavon, The Monkey in Me

They were the Great Generation. Because of them and all that they were, he had learned to love Hong Kong.

Leon, to his everlasting credit, made a point every Sunday of taking his Mother out to a nice Sunday Dim-sum or Buffet Lunch. He would and could never forget her sacrifice that had made his life. This deep humility and remembrance are a key part of Hong Kong, which you could never see. But it could be felt in the wind. The sweat and tears of sacrifice are still in the air. They are tears that have been transformed into undying love and respect, becoming the most beautiful eternal perfume that could ever grace a place. Thankfulness still means something here.

Leon was already having a drink. It was going to be a good night. He was honoured that Leon was his friend. It was not the normal foreigner and Hong Kong person relationship. Leon treated him like a fellow Chinese, the way they treat each other with respect and friendship. It was nice.

Thank God he was away from ArthurRichard and Eric Johnson Parker. Tonight would be fun.

""Leon, How are you?"

"Same as always. Not very good. Business is down."

"Same for me, too. The Year of the Rat is really bad. Earthquakes, Typhoons and Floods. Next we will be seeing Dragons on the Mountains."

"Ha, Ha . . . that''s funny! So, tonight, is it Vodka or Absinthe?"

"Oh, let'slet's go for the Absinthe! I want to think."

"I knew you would say that. Tthat'shat's what I am drinking already."

"Leon, look at her. What do you think?"?"

A tall Filipina had just entered the bar, smiled at another foreigner and sat down at the bar.

""Looks OK. More like your type, Bobby?"

65

"No, not really. You know I am pretty busy with the Ghost in China."."

The Ghost was what he called HER, #7. The Chinese believe ghosts can attach themselves to your soul and then they are very hard to shake off.

""Yes, you have changed a lot. Must be your mid-life crisis. You are so faithful."

"Yes, that is true. I have changed. I am having a mid-life crisis. Pretty pathetic isn'tisn't it?"

"No, not really. I guess you need this."

"Yes, it is true. I was getting pretty sick of not having anyone. Empty sex means nothing to me now."

"It's all good, Bobby. But never say 'never'."."

He looked over at three Russian Girls. A little worse for wear, he thought. But he said, ""Yes, never say 'never'."."

The Absinthe and Red Bull was hitting them both. Seventy percent proof Absinthe had caused Van Gogh to cut off his ear and had only been legal again in Europe for the past several years. It warmed you up and made you think, which could be a dangerous thing. Other Alcohol helped you avoid thinking.

The Bar was filling up. Businessmen. Rugby players. Girls arriving in small groups. Filipinas here. Indonesian girls. And there, a few mainland girls. The disco music was throbbing.

""As usual, no Chinese guys except you, Leon. What is the problem here?"

"Yes, you know the story. They have their places, we have ours. Hard to get to know these foreigners. They never learn about Chinese culture or Hong Kong. For them it'sit's just business. This is their play and for us it is home. They come and go and we stay. East Meets West. You know the phrase."

"Pretty bad if you ask me. Like, why are they here? Hong Kong means everything to me."

"You're You're different, Bobby. Have another Absinthe."!"

It was true and very embarrassing. There were no Chinese in the bar. Just Nepalese waiters, Expats, and Girls from out of town. Hong Kong was a very limited melting-pot and had been that way since it was first administered by the British in the early 1840s. This was not always true, but largely so. It just took a long time for both parties to know each other and simply took great time and effort and perhaps decades to reach a mutual cultural understanding. Most of the Westerners would leave for other placeson before that happened.

Separate lives and separate parties. To be with the Chinese, you had to become one. To be with the Foreigners, you had to become one. As natural as it seemed, going native was hard. Getting to know a culture of six thousand years was also very hard. It took lots of time and effort. Sometimes it was hard to switch back to the Foreign channels after being with the Chinese for months.

""Yes, Leon, I love Hong Kong and detest those people. But they should make some effort to learn about Chinese ways?"

"They never do. So we just ignore them."..."

In fact, it was true. A couple of the rugby players were looking at Leon, not with disdain but with a," "What is the Chinese guy here for"" look.

Nothing intense, just a glance now and then.

It was a real modern United Nations. Brits with Brits, Aussies with Aussies. Indians with Indians. Arabs with Arabs.

All so very tribal.

Stick with your group. They are the ones you can understand. How many of us only have friends from the same tribe we are in? It is so common as to be ridiculous. We just don'tdon't know how to mix with other peoples.

If you want to see how out of touch most of the expatriates are in Hong Kong, or anywhere for that matter, go up to the neighbourhood called "Mid-Levels" about 5pm any day.

Try Conduit Road and go for a stroll. This is where many of the rich oblivious expatriates live. Just take a walk. See the Filipino and Indonesian maids walking the Expat'sExpats' dogs, and taking their children out to play. Go down one road and see the wine shop and delicatessen. They are living lives completely separated from the reality that feeds them. They can'tcan't speak Chinese and could be anywhere else. China means nothing to them. It is just a place to make their money. It was really noses stuck up in the air. Again, thisThis was not his Hong Kong any more.

Out of touch and Drunk.

This was not their playground. The Chinese were not their servants any more.

""Yes, Leon it is true, but things are hard to understand. Look at me and the Ghost. I want love and she just wants security. It'sIt's just not very romantic."

"Good point. The Mainland girls first want security. Love is not fast like in the West. It is slow and based on many years of mutual love. You just need to understand it. This is why I almost never have sex with my wife, Bobby. At least you still get some. Ha, Ha."

"Leon, have another drink, too complicated.".""

The bar was really filling up. Some dancing. Guys downing drinks. Chatting up the girls. But this was not let's-get-to-know-each-other chatting. It was guy-checking-out-the-body chatting. How-Much-Money-for-the-night chatting. Where-are-you-staying chatting.

Two Thai and one Filipina Girls were looking at him and Leon who, with his six-foot frame was a good-looking guy. After a while you could tell where people were from. It'sIts not true that, ""They all look the same." ". Asia is amazing for its beautiful faces and mixtures. Takes time to appreciate, but really worth it.

Filipinas with some Spanish Blood and Arab blood, mixed with Malay.

Tall Northern-Chinese Girls.

Petite Thais.

It was always amazing to see.

Just think of where they were! He and Leon were located in the center of a five city block area. About five thousand girls and one thousand guys were there together. Forget your struggle for sex. Guys had the advantage. There was something so easy about it all. As one good friend had told him once, ""I want them to come to me."". And this was the situation here. If you smiled they came up to you.

Heaven for men.

As the music boomed and the strobe lights flashed to give the right Disco movement, the veiled intent of the night became alive. The girls pushed and the guys gave way.

When he looked at them he tried to imagine the distant village in a distant province. He could see the blue sky over the farms, the water buffalo on the side of a rice field that had been their home. Perhaps somewhere a small motherless child was being cared for by a grandmother, and rice cooking in the small kitchen, smoke rising from a wooden fire.

It was so easy to separate that reality from the fantasy of the disco. We all have lives and this was just a short vacation from them. He often wondered why so many of us were here. The Victims and Victimizers. Or were we all victims of a game none of us understood until too late?

He thought about #7 and how much she meant to him. But that would end soon if only there was a way.

Many of the girls were educated, here for short stays to make some money and back home again. Others had borrowed money to come and had to work for a year. If there was a Trade Show in town or the Seventh Fleet in the harbour business was good. But it was business.

This week it was the Jewellery Show and things were just peachy. One look at all those watches and rings and he wanted to put on his sunglasses or go surfing near the Kennedy compound.

While there were some real relationships that developed, they were few and far between. Sometimes you got so drunk you couldn'tcouldn't remember anything and the morning was a mystery of regret. Other times, sadly, the sex was terrible. Other times you could not remember where you had been.

Every once and a while you felt something.

Leon called over the three girls.

""Leon, I am retired."

"Have another drink, Bobby!.""

Outside the Typhoon made its first heavy blow.

""This Typhoon is something, Leon. We might be here all night."

"Good, then I won'twon't need to go home."

""Hello, Guys! Having fun? I am Rita."."

The three girls sat down and smiled.

Rita was the tallest, with a big chest and pretty dress on.—Sexy. The other two were older, still pretty, but life was beginning to weigh on them.

""Where are you girls from? "?" Leon asked, smiling like a Leopard.

Once again, Rita spoke up. ""I am from the Philippines, and Asia and Ri are from Thailand. Can we get a drink?"?"

""Sure, what do you want?",?" said Leon.

"Tequila for all of us. Is that OK?"

"Sure."."

Looking over at the waitress who had appeared out of nowhere, the Tequilas were on the way.

Rita was looking at him, and asked Leon, ""Why is your friend so sad?"

"He is always like this. Wait till later..."!"

A real ice-breaker.

He was not sad. Leon was acting weird too. He never brought girls over. Something must be going on with him. Before Leon could speak, he replied instead..

""No, I am not sad. I am just relaxing. I had a long day.".."

Rita put her hand on his lap.

""Oh, I understand, Darling. Me, too."

"Thanks for understanding."."

The drinks arrived for the Girls.

""Have another drink, Leon. Here'sHere's to the Typhoon!"

""Cheers, Bobby"!"

The girls were too busy downing their drinks to hear.

The second girl, Asia, put her hand on Leon'sLeon's knee.

""Leon, is that your name? Can we have another round, please?"?"

Leon called for another round and more absinthe for all of us. The girls told us their life stories. Ri was recently divorced and had a son to support. Asia was here for the first time and really liked Leon. Rita was a former school-teacher with a University degree, trying to pay for a liver operation for her mother. While they were talking, Leon was getting really drunk. He never drank like this.

In Chinese, he asked Leon, "What's"What's going on, Leon? You never drink like this."

""Long story.. I will tell you later."."

Some time later another foreigner came over to talk to us. He was a tall strong Russian, Andrei, who for some reason was wearing a name card saying simply, "Andrei, Russia". He must have been eyeing the third Thai Girl, Ri, from a distance. He smiled and sat down.

""Oh you'reyou're an American, I heard your accent. Thanks for messing up the world economy. "."

'"No, he's from Hong Kong,"," Leon chimed in.

""Thanks, Leon for the support! No, Andrei, I am glad Russia is doing so well. We all like Putin."

71

"Me, too. He is a great man."

"What are you doing in Hong Kong, Andrei?"

"I am buying USB Flash. Do you know any good sources?"

"I sell lots of those, Andrei."."

Reaching into his pocket, he gave Andrei his card.

Andrei took it, smiled and grabbing Ri's hand rushed off to the dance floor. On his way, he crumpled the card and tossed it on the floor.

""Have another drink, Leon!"!"

You too, Bobby."."

Rita and Asia were happily drinking even more tequila.   Asia went to the Ladies Room. Rita went too, and then Leon went off to chase a Russian girl by the bar. He was pretty drunk too. Out of the corner of his eye, he saw John Graham, an old friend.

""Hey, Johnny! What'sWhat's going on?"

"Oh the Communist Chinese guy is back."."

Graham was a long-haired Englishman, Indian-shirt-wearing, looking like some sort of hippy, with a strong resemblance to the new James Bond guy, except for the hair. . Strange type, he was always seen with older Asian women. He had been married, but then divorced. A bad traffic accident on a typhoon night just like today had left a red scar on his forehead. A former British paratrooper, he was not one to be trifled with. In fact everyone was afraid of him. He treated the foreigners with disdain and was only out for the sex. He would leave at 12 midnight, sharp, with a different girl every night.

""What are you drinking, mate?"

"Absinthe, Graham, what else?"

"Going for it, eh? Crazy American Special Forces Officer! Go for it, Mate!"

"You bet! The Typhoon is coming. You love Typhoons, my Friend."!"

A frown on Graham'sGraham's face. Then he gave a big smile.

"Why don'tdon't you go driving tonight, Bobby? Then we can look the same. You really are a bastard."

"Not really a Bastard. Jerk or Fool would be a better description. I like the Scar. You can tell everyone it was from the Falklands War."

"Yes, 'jerk' does sound better. Did you hear about the next war?"

"No. YGraham,ou mean the US attacking Iran?"

"No. China is going to attack India."

"Really? Why?"

"Well, first of all they need to get some practice. Taiwan is too hard for a first one. They want the Indian state of Arunchal, which is mineral-rich and supposedly part of Tibet. Even the Dalai Lama says so."

"Wouldn'tWouldn't that go Nuclear, Graham?"

"No. Probably not. Probably they'd fire some missiles at Chengdu, and Northern India."

"I thought India was pretty strong."

"Everyone is afraid of you Communists, Bobby. The Indians would be fighting up-hill again like in 1962."

"Wow, Graham, you still remember the 1962 war! Nehru was a jerk to Chou En Lai."

"Sure was. But China is much stronger now. ' Cake Walk' or 'Slam Dunk' as your Americans love to say right before you walk into shit."

"Interesting, Graham! Have a drink! Better yet, get yourself some Absinthe! Might clear your head. And don'tdon't forget the Korea problem! China and the US will have to co-operate on this one. But not sure if that will blow before or after our next great depression."

"Thinking about doing that, Bobby. Be right back. You know I need to find my victim for tonight."

"Sure, Graham. There is a little Kim Jong Il in all of us, you freaky vampire. See you later."."

Surveying the room to find Leon, he first spotted Andrei doing some suck mouth and ass grab with Ri. That was going to happen. It was a bit strange because Andrei

73

was so damn tall and Ri so short. He had to bend at an almost a ninety degrees angle to kiss her and how he got his hand on her ass was beyond logic. Leon was still drinking and talking to the Russian Brunette. Graham was getting his drink and talking loudly to some Indian guy about the next war. The Indian guy was in for a tongue-lashing. Graham could be really awful to those he did not know.

Outside, the Typhoon was raging, raining so hard you could not go outside. So he was stuck. Asia and Rita were dancing with some well-dressed Europeans probably from the Netherlands, judging by the overdone Orange Shirts. At the Bar, a short American was arguing with the Nepalese Bar-tender about the value of Gold, and shouting at the top of his lungs that he knew where the economy was going. The Bartender had better listen to him.

Just another night in Wan Chai.

His phone. HER. #7. The Ghost.

What was he doing out so late? Why was he drunk? Did he have a girl in Hong Kong? When was he coming back? Where was the money? Then she hung up.

Love. wasn'tWasn't it just so much understanding and caring?

He called her back. Predictably the phone was now turned off.

Leon came back, this time with a Russian girl and one bottle of Champagne.

""Bobby, this is Irina. She'sShe's from Ukraine. Nice Girl."

"Leon, don'tdon't drink too much. I don'tdon't want your wife looking for you."

"No problem. Sshe'sshe's in Thailand."

"Oh, you didn'tdidn't tell me."

"You didn'tdidn't ask. Ha. Ha. Have another drink! Do you want Champagne, Bobby?"?"

Now this was really strange. Leon would never buy Champagne for someone. Something was wrong and he would probably never find out.

""Thanks, Leon. I will stick to the Absinthe. Getting some good thinking in."

"Yes. Me, too.".."

Leon grabbed Irina'sIrina's thigh way up. "Irina's"Irina's friend is available over there. Should I bring her?"

"No, not yet, Leon. Need more absinthe. You know I have a conscience and need to get real drunk to forget about the Ghost."

"What, your friend does not want a girl?"?" asked Irina.

""No, he has screwed them all Baby. ALL of them."" He took particular pleasure when he said the "ALL".

""In China they call Bobby, "Sun Wu Kong"—"The Monkey King"..

"Monkeys get lots of sex in China?"

"This one does all the time. Why, he has 4four kids and two wives already and counting."

"Oh, impressive! Must cost a lot.""

"Really rich guy." ."

Irina gave him a more impressed look. Irina'sIrina's friend gave him a smile. Ri and Andrei stumbled out of the bar into the Typhoon, his hand still defying the laws of physics on her ass. Graham and the Indian guy were arguing. The short American was causing a scene telling everyone that the bar-tender was calling him a liar and only he knew what was going on. The Nepalese bouncers were moving in.

Hands on his shoulder to tell him to calm down.

He left in a huff and into the most amazing rain storm. The Nepalese Bartender shook his head and poured another Absinthe for Graham.

It was now One Thirty a.m. It was still very early. You could party until Ten a.m. in Wan Chai. This was really just the start of the night.

In one corner he saw another friend, Saad.

Saad was a Jordanian Palestinian. He told everyone he was from Turkey so that he did not have to say much more. He was a Moslem, but he did drink beer. Forty-ish and very rich, he had a brick factory in Jordan and was related to some big Fatah leader. He both hated and admired Hezbollah. But Jordan was his home and he wanted nothing to do with Palestinian politics. One of his partners, Ben Rochman, was an Israeli and they got along fine. Ben was a happy-go-lucky fellow. Saad was really really serious.

" "More Haram for you, Saad? Where is Ben?"

"Ben is out of town. And yes, I just want to see how you imperialists live. ."

"Well, ask the new King. He knows better than me."

"Yes, I forgot you have become Chinese. At least this King has not killed us like his Father. And well, after thirty years we are part of the scenery now. Though I must say the last wife was more than we could deal with."

"Yes. I saw her on CNN with Larry King. She reminds me of is someone who never grew up. Peter Pan with a Palace. SaadSaid, Ramadan is starting soon. How can you be drinking at a time like this?"

"You know how it is."

Saad was always good for some conversation. Since he, Bobby, had studied Islamic History at University he always knew that Saad would keep him up to date on the Middle East.

Ever since the Iraq War had started he refused to go to any Moslem countries, mostly because he was ashamed of the war without reason that we had launched on Iraq.

And it was shame. The last thing they needed in any of these countries was more Americans. That is what he loved about China. He could not influence them. They would influence him and he would always be a minority."

"When were you last back home, Saad?"

"Last month, we now call Amman, 'little Baghdad'."

"That many Iraqis live there now?"

"Yes, it is a flood."

"But I thought the American Surge was working?"

"What Surge? They hate all of you. The only ones happy are the Iranians. Your soldiers stay in the bases and eat Burger King. There is no fighting any more because all you do is bribe everyone. It is hard to get killed when you do nothing. That is why the violence is down. Don'tDon't believe anything General Petreaus says. He is getting out while the getting out is good. It'sIt's all bullshit, all of it."

"How is this going to end?"

"Well it'sit's obvious. We will have a strong Iran and fleeing Americans. Just like Vietnam. Peace with Honour. The way your dollar is going, it might be worse. You simply cannot afford all this crap any more. But no-one realizes this. Bush has just made things worse for all of us. Next, Egypt will explode too, and then Pakistan. We can'tcan't all move to Oklahoma, you know. Bush is an idiot and Cheney is really like a Devil. Americans are hated, and hated with a passion. You are finished in the region for the next 30thirty years."

"Well a lot of us agree with you...But Israel might attack Iran?".

"Yes, is that before or after Pakistan explodes? Let them go ahead and try. Then there will be no world economy ever again. It will be back to the Caves for all of us. This is a real mess, Bobby. No solution in sight. Why did you guys elect Bush? He has been a disaster for mankind."

"I understand.—Many of us agree with you.—Saad, have a good party! Maybe it won'twon't be so bad in the end. We are lost now. Maybe we will all find our way later. Remember Moses in the Desert and Mohammed in Medina. Things might change."

"You are right. And thanks, Bobby. See you next time you are in town."

With that Bobby went over to Leon. He was always like this with foreigners. The only ones he was comfortable with were Chinese.

A new crowd was coming in, more for the dancing than the drinking.

Absinthe does not make you drunk, until the one moment that you don'tdon't remember. That moment had not come. Looking at Leon, he remembered he was the Monkey King, the guy who could change shapes, and defy even the Gods in Heaven and Hell. But then again, after all his stunts, they put a big mountain on top of his head for five hundred years, until Guan Ying, the Goddess of Mercy let him out of the mountain. The Mountain was still pressing down on his back. Where was the Goddess tonight?

Another couple came and sat down; a tall Hispanic guy, wearing his Nike Golf shirt and hugging his Filipina girl-friend.

""I heard you talking before. Where are you from in the States? I am from Texas."

Leon spoke up again, more slurred this time.

""No.—He is Chinese, from Hong Kong, can'tcan't you see."?"

Leon was always defending him, as if he understood that they were both fish out of water when the Foreigners were around. The noodle-shop was their last refuge in modern Hong Kong.

""Thanks, Leon. Hi! My name is Bobby. What's yours?"

"I am Ricardo, from Austin""

""You look Mexican to me,"," Leon was on a roll.

""Leon, Texas—where Ricardo is from—used to be in Mexico."

Ricardo gave Leon a confused look.

""Ricardo, what brings you to Hong Kong?

"You are the first person to be so nice. I am here for the first time for the Jewellery Show at the Convention

Centre.—What do you think of Maria? She'sShe's my new girl friend."

"Good catch, especially for your first time."

"Yes. Hey, by the way, how much should I pay her? I really don'tdon't know. In Las Vegas it'sit's two hundred dollars per night."

"Well you need to ask her—about one thousand Hong Kong Dollars should do it. Give her more if you like her. She probably could use the money to send back home. Be nice to her and she will be nice to you. Same as anywhere else."

"Thanks, what was your name?"

"Bobby. Thanks, Ricardo. Good Luck."

"Thanks, Bobby. Maybe I will see you here tomorrow. This place is great. You sure know a lot." ."

The scene kept changing but staying the same. Graham came over to ask about travel visas. Leon left later with Irina. He sat there sometimes alone but never alone. Just the way he liked it.

Alone in a crowd.

Eyeing all the girls, sizing them up.

Watching couples newly formed leave into the night. Soon things began to blur.

The blurring was getting bad. A tall man stumbled up to shake his hand. It was Eric Johnson Parker, his client. With him was a tall black girl also very, very drunk. They were both stumbling.

""Hey, Eric! You didn'tdidn't call."

"Sorry, I forgot."

"Thought you were not drinking."

"ScrewFuck You."

With that he slumped and was carried out by the Tall Black girl. Wow, even Eric was on the way down these days. But Eric was not the only one confused.

Imprints on our Minds V

M.A.S.H will never end.
Contract with America.
Manuel Noriega and John McCain'sMcCain's wife.
APAC in Peru. I just love it when the Leaders wear the local clothes.
Bangladesh
The Nepalese Communist Party.
 FRIENDS…what a great show! That is how we really are. Dinosaur Specialists are everywhere and they try to pick up waitresses at the Pizza place.
CNN 360 covers all the news. Anderson Cooper wears CNN Blazers and Struts.
You want to see things from 360 degrees. I want to see what'swhat's inside.
 Bill Maher was terrible for being critical of the bombing of Afghanistan.
Muslims are dangerous.
Get that Border Fence up now.
Real Estate and Banking are great careers, and Lawyers can'tcan't be trusted.
Heartland of America—where is that?
NASCAR is the fastest growing sport.
JaipurJodpur at night . . . boom.
Going 90 on Highway 5 at night. LA is so close.
 Guns create violence, Guns are our right.
The Nuclear family is the best, we all should have one.
Abortion is a right, Abortion is murder.
 Indiana Jones does not get old, but ET can get home-sick.
Top Gun is a feel-good movie.
The American Military is the world'sworld's greatest force.

Caleb Kavon, The Monkey in Me

Tony Blair solves the Middle East'sEast's problems—
he is not discredited.
 We should have bombed Hanoi and Beijing when we
had the chance.
RFK'sRFK's funeral .
We need Health Insurance. We don'tdon't need
Health Insurance.
Send another Brigade to Afghanistan—that will solve
the problem.
Pakistan has a population of 164 million Moslems.
Bangladesh has a population of 150 million Moslems.
Indonesia has a population of 234 million souls. Most
of them are Moslem.
Did they bomb the Sheraton or the Inter-Continental?
Hummers are great vehicles and a status symbol
along with white BMWs and three-bedroom homes.
Just don'tdon't drive them in Iraq.
Bob Hope was a great American, Frank Sinatra was
not.
Texaco and Shell.
Country Music is from Nashville.
 Everyone who likes country music wants to drive a
Pick-Up Truck ..
 Shake and Bake, and Antacid.
Salsa.
 Rolex is the watch , and Google is a great stock to
watch.
 We are all overweight.
The Oklahoma City Bombing never happened.
Waco.
Watergate and Cheney .
The Oil Man.
 The Marlboro' Man.
 High School Football on Fridays, College on
Saturday and NFL on Sunday. Monday, the office
pool and productivity is up.
English Premier League.

Caleb Kavon, The Monkey in Me

Beckham and Company.
Like so what?
 Screaming Eagles.
Mommy Dearest.
 Break the Glass Ceiling.
Mothers against Drunk Driving and COPS.
The MBA is a ticket to Corporate Success.
I can'tcan't use Excel, never learned.
The Surge is working in Iraq.
Mixed Marriages in Wassilla Alaska.
 The Last Great Generation.
The Next Great Depression.
 Egypt is a democracy and Syria is not.
JOE SIXPACK is a real person and he votes.
Now it is Joe the Plumber.
God Help Us.

Hypocrisy

He woke up that morning with Rita naked at his side. When and how he had returned, he could not remember. He checked his money, his valuables, all was intact. His body had no bruises.

Not good.

Rita was sleeping like a baby. At least he remembered her name. That was a good sign, in an otherwise state of absolute confusion bordering on panic.

What had happened last night?

This was not the first time. And each time he said it would be last. Drinking was an issue. But this was not Leavingleaving Las Vegas. He did not drink every day, and would not drink in the daylight hours. Sometimes he would go weeks without drinking.

But it was binge drinking.

Major drinking in one event.

He did not have a headache, but was tired as hell. Absinthe does not give headaches, or digestion issues. He knew from experience that it would take one day to recuperate.

Checking the time, it was 10am. Red Bull does that to you. You sleep lightly and wake up. He looked in the mirror.

Looking bad.

Hair all up in the air.

Yellow Eyes—like a wolf.

Looking back to the Bed.—He could not believe his eyes and he felt really guilty.

The Typhoon was still at full blast now. Signs were falling and he could see some garbage-cans rolling.

Some momentary gaps in the wind, which meant the Typhoon was on its way somewhere else like the three minute stop of a train at the Berlin Main Railway Station. It would be ending soon. Typhoons had a beginning, middle and end.

The first rush of wind, intensifying.

The eye.

A calm that made all things seeable and the final blow as tons of rain rushed through with a dying wind. It would be over, and then on again in a short while, with it.

The Solstice had come and gone. The Typhoon would soon leave their lives.

Looking back at the bed and the sleeping Rita, he could only wonder.

Yes, this was the point of it all.

Hypocrisy or no Hypocrisy?

Was this a relationship or just sex? This was the question. Not frigging to be or not to be. Since he could not remember it anyway, probably it was nothing.

Can you confess to something you do not remember?

Did we take off our clothes? What was it like anyway? Here was another human being, lying with him. Was it going to be one of those, "Here's"Here's your money, Thanks a lot. Give me your number. Bye."."

Probably.

What was he doing? Number Seven was the center of his life. He had no need for this Rita. At least he remembered her name.

Another poor Third World Girl, victimized by the marauding hordes of visitors.

Another Middle-aged man victimized by his own lack of sense.

She would get her money. What was in it for him?

Not how life was supposed to be. He was as guilty as CNN and the Air Guitar Guy.Larry King. This was one big Air Guitar totally undeserving of mercy. What do you have if your main focus is on relationships and you cannot even get that right?

The Buddhists know that all is suffering. You are born and live to die in pain. The young women in your life also pass to old age. What you loved so dearly will pass away. Even the greatest passion and love will slowly cool. Your brain keeps you craving what you don'tdon't have. Crack-addicts and Love-addicts are cousins.

He turned on the TV. Oh, no! Jurassic Park.

Just what he needed to relax.—Dinosaurs hunting humans.

Thankfully it was ending. The heroes, loading into ato helicopter after successfully escaping renegade reborn dinosaurs. The next movie was even worse.

SPANGLISH with Adam Sandler.

Lots of holes in this one.

Rich Very Upper Class Family takes on a Mexican maid. Then the family gives an opportunity to the Maid'sMaid's daughter while the wife is having an affair and is never home. Meanwhile Adam falls in love with maid, is left with nothing when the Maid leaves, maintaining her pride. Nice houses, empty lives.

Like we should ask… What happens to Maid after the film? What happens to Adam and his cheating wife and miserable home life? What happens to his restaurant that he has learned to hate?

God, he was sure that thinking was the first Sin. It was not Eve biting the apple. That was just something done by reflex. Thinking was definitely the first sin.

First call of the day.

Hermann, his German customer, was in town. Could he see him? Later.

A business proposal for him.

Had a long night last night, Hermann, you know how it is. Please wait till I call, I will be there in the late afternoon.

Second Call of the Day

HER. #7.

This time, really frantic.

Where was the money? Look it's Sunday. Can'tCan't send yet. Her Father could die, what was I doing? Nothing.

He looked over to Rita who was beginning to wake up. This was serious.

Where were you? I still havehad one meeting tomorrow, then I willhe would send the money. Bye.

Not good enough. This was getting out of hand.

"Rita."

""Good Morning, Darling. How did you sleep? You were very romantic last night."

"I was? Don'tDon't remember much."

"You came over and got me and told me I was the most beautiful thing you ever saw."

"I did? Must have been the alcohol. Last time I saw you, you were dancing."

"Later I came over. You were alone, still looking sad. Do you always speak Chinese when you have sex?"

"I was talking Chinese?"

"Yes. You were. I thought it was sexy."

"Wow! Really can'tcan't remember a thing."

"You were fine, until you started to call someone on the phone. Then you got mad."."

"He looked for his phone. Yes, at 5.30am he had been calling HER, #7."

""Sorry, Rita. Not sure what I was doing. I usually—I mean, recently—I haven'thaven't been picking up girls in Wan Chai. I have a very serious girlfriend in China. Really, I am sorry. I am not that way. Believe me. You look like a great person and deserve better."

"It'sIt's OK. You'reYou're a great guy, and good in bed."

"I am? I haven'thaven't heard that for a while. Thanks. All Very Kind of you."

"Look Rita, Let'slet's sleep a little so I can recover after such activity and wait for the Typhoon to pass. We can eat later. OK?"

"Very funny. You are very romantic."."

And, with that she was back in his arms listening and watching some movie with the girl from FRIENDS

86

who was married to Brad Pitt. This film was even worse. The plot was stupid.

A happy couple stage a ridiculous fight about washing the dishes and end up selling their house. You need to work hard to destroy a relationship so quickly. All the same it was a good commentary on selfishness, but hardly realistic. People try hard to stay together, especially women.

But that was Hollywood. We had Spielberg and only Spielberg. The diet was monotonous and we had bought into it.

Bad Movies and Bad Plots from the ""imagination guys,"" flood our cinemas. Batman #20 will be on soon. They have nothing new to say. They want things to sell so badly that they don'tdon't care about what they sell. Sounds familiar? And, we want to buy so badly we don'tdon't care what we buy.

It was the start of another Day in the Desert. The world was burning and we had The Bone.Motley Crue. So here he was with another girl.

All was going well. She liked him. What a mistake. They all start liking him like that. If she was sane she would get out of there right immediately. No problem getting women to marry him. Three marriages showed that. The problem was him. The song by Carly Simon,", "Will You Still Love Me Tomorrow?;"" was written about him.

It was not fear of commitment; it was never keeping his word. Something was always better on the other side. Or they couldn'tcouldn't make him happy. Why do we always depend on someone else?

He was a poor excuse of a man and husband. Judging from last night in Wan Chai, he was not the only hypocrite in the neighbourhood. But this had gone too far. He was disgusted with himself. He was better than this. How could he change?

This was his mid-life crisis.

He desired the relationship he had never had. He wanted to end the lies. Kill the Story. This is me. This is what I am like. This is what I do. If he didn'tdidn't have responsibilities, he would just like to run off to Brazil. That was a cop-out too. He couldn'tcouldn't run away. He needed to fix himself where he stood and stop making excuses for everything.

He loved HER—#7—and wanted it to work. But he thought it probably was going to go nowhere.

This was a good first step. Absinthe works.

He felt a bit better.

Rita said she was busy and soon left. Yes, she knew, too. This was not going to be anything special. He was not the one. She did not even leave her phone number, and he did not even ask.

Hermann Hesse

He loved to be with educated Germans. They were so analytical; definitely liberal and with a clear view on the world. Of course modern Germany was undergoing severe changes again.

High unemployment, decreasing security and having to mix with the rest of Europe.

Once again the heart was there. The world'sworld's problems were largely economic, but very real and imposing. Big changes were needed now. We were on the cusp of a big revolution.

The Typhoon had ended. Hermann Franks was waiting for him in the lobby. Short, fat, and well dressed with very short hair, he was the last of the German Upper Class. He had those blue-grey eyes and the look of success.

Educated in the Best Schools, beneficiary of the booming Germany of the 70s and 80s, his company was now struggling to make ends meet. Inflation was biting and he had trouble keeping up with salaries. A Buddhist, he was just coming in from three weeks in Thailand at a monastery. He was an old and very good friend.

" "Ah, Bobby, man, how are you? Long time no see. Still struggling with your demons and trying to change the world?"

"Yes, I am the original rebel without a cause, Hermann. Had a tough one last night."

"Yes, before I was a Buddhist, I suffered a few of those with you."

"Yes, Hermann, you were a killer. Vodka martinis all the way. Remember the whore-house in Hamburg? Or when we insulted the Bavarian Chancellor at the Computer Show? You wanted to steal his cell-phone. That was great."

"That is all past now, Bobby. Three weeks in a temple is good for curing the soul."

"I imagine. Sign me up! But what do you think, Hermann, about this Reincarnation thing?"

"Bobby, you are the obvious case for it. Why do you have so many relationships with women? Why do you? Don'tDon't you feel as if you were with these people before? Then why do you leave them for something else? You seem to know them all, and seem to know where you need to be, though you have obviously never quite found the final spot on your path."

"All True, Hermann."

"Freedom is when you quit trying to be someone or something. When you no longer define yourselves by others; be it by your position, income or aspirations. Bobby, you are always angry and can'tcan't let go of the absurdity of the world. You are too concrete and not concrete enough at the same time. Leave it alone for a change. You are right about so much, but it punishes you all the same."

"Well, not always, Hermann, but you are right-on. I have been a bit pushed out the last couple of days. Nice to hear such counsel."

"Had the Best Times of my life with you in the past. No-one has parties like you. No-one opens up like you. You are not afraid of letting people know you as you are. You taught me a lot. I got divorced because of you."

"What?"

"I was miserable before with Margaritte. I saw you changing your life at the drop of a hat and decided I could do it too. We actually have a better relationship now and the kids are happier."

"I didn'tdidn't know. You didn'tdidn't say anything at all."

"I couldn't.I couldn't. Just like you, I tend to disappear when changing. Just like a butterfly.—When the change is complete, everyone can see it. We all disappear sometimes to the deepest depths just to avoid the sun. I imagine you are in the depths now. The night is your only friend."

"Good Metaphor. I am still in the cocoon and it is strangling me every day. Not feeling real peaceful now. Kind of disturbed. I have another failing relationship. Not sure why this always happens to me. Yes, it is true. I love the night."

"It'sIt's not your first cocoon, Bobby. I have seen at least three in the past ten years. Tough transformations. But I am sure this next one will be the best so far."

"Yes, everyone has seen me change radically. Cocooning is tough."

"When you forget who you are, who you love, and who you hate, that will be real progress. Wait for it. It is coming. You have so many questions that can'tcan't be answered. Just stop asking them and start living. Life is a dream."

He felt a smile coming to his lips and some peace. The silence was a friend. Hermann smiled too. A moment of realization crossed them both.

""I have a meditation meeting now, Bobby. See you. Jorg from my office will send your orders next week. Try not to screw them up? OK? You just need some time to work these issues out. When the cocoon opens you will feel better. Stop struggling. I know that it is hard for you, but it will work out."

"Sure, Hermann. Thanks a lot. You gave me a lot to think about. Bye. I love you."

"I love you too, Bobby.".""

With that, he left. Hard as it was, imagining this, Hermann was now a teacher of peace.

The good feeling left after a while. Though hopeful, his life had no place in the Da Vinci code, no exciting chase for the Holy Grail. All that Hermann had said was probably true. He needed to make the change.

Where to start?

Caleb Kavon, The Monkey in Me

He did feel more optimistic and happy now. Must have been the new orders Hermann was giving him. Hong Kong had always given him so much. It was his town— good, bad and indifferent. Surveying the endless in-and-out of the hotel, it was suddenly not as threatening. Maybe he could change himself.

Tin Hau Temple

He wanted to get some air, and took a walk down Nathan Road. Sunday evening was coming down. The crowds were leaving the restaurants. Sunday is family day in Hong Kong. Most families go out together, taking their Mothers and Fathers out for a good dinner. It is a happy time.

There will be Mah Jong at night and good fruits and the local TV show.

It was a beautiful sight, children escorting Grandma into the restaurant, the waiters bringing everyone'severyone's favourite food. Couples were walking seriously through the night; discussing the week ahead and their futures. The newspaper salesmen, with their blue-green booths or overhead awnings, were fanning themselves. There was a stray cat here and there. The streets were crowded but peaceful and not loud.

The Sweet and Bitter smell of the Chinese medicine shop mixed equally with the steam coming out of the vents of noodle shops. This is a walk that all should make and appreciate. You begin to know China here, in the sweat of the long night at their side. Six Thousand years and you are lucky enough to be with them here and now.

So different from the lost sense of Wan Chai

One Sunday night in an eternity. Maybe it was some sort of Karma. He had been transported to be with them so long ago and they still gave more than he could ever give in return.

There she was, Tin Hau—the goddess of the Fishermen and women.—She would provide safety from the storms of the sea and bring all back to safety. In the old days, the Temple had been very close to the sea, but reclamation now made it so far. A beach and village had once been there. Silence, a more simple life, and the shouts of the fishermen had been the music played to waves on the beach. The Goddess had seen it all and still divined the fortunes of many.

The retirees in the small plaza in front played Chinese chess and smoked in their white sleeveless T-shirts and shorts with black socks. That was style. Give me one of them over a Paris Cat-walk any time.

Simple humanity over the illusion of cool. The old men had nothing to prove and nowhere to go.

As a boy they had given him lessons in Chinese chess and bought him soft drinks, teasing and praising his every move. Good friends and so gentle to him. In his heart he could hug every one of them and never leave their sides. They were so amazing. He loved them more than anyone could ever know. He loved this place. He loved these people.

Entering the temple he got 3three incense sticks and lit them. Bowing down he looked straight at the Goddess and thanked Her for so many blessings. She would protect him as she had protected precious Hong Kong. She would give him the lucky breaks he needed to survive and somehow break out of the doldrums. Tin Hau would help him merge the past and the present. For these blessings he would never leave her, despite last night.

He walked happily back to the hotel, and unhappily entered the fake world of the Lobby.

Sleep.

Tomorrow was China, his home in the Desert.

Journey to the East

At 6am he left Shangri La. He was crossing over.

A journey from Hong Kong to China is a dramatic event. You leave the cover of the pseudo-western world and enter another world. One quarter of mankind is waiting for you. It is another world and another political system. They have never heard of Larry King, Bill Maher, the Bone and David Bowie, though they have all heard of Kobe Bryant and Yao Ming.

They watch the dull Meetings of the Communist party where everyone sits and listens. They dream of Brand Names and always have a calculator at their side.

Most Chinese don'tdon't speak English or watch CNN. People often make the mistake of thinking that the Westernized Chinese who speak English represent Chinese thinking of today.

Wrong.

China is so complicated that what we call Western concepts are shared really by just a minute fraction of the people. Here people hark back to their hometowns, and traditions. Different age groups have completely different perceptions of the world. Different economic classes look at things differently. Different cities, towns and counties are ruled completely differently. There are one million rules which can be followed at any time. Leave Shanghai, Shenzhen and Beijing where most westerners stay and you are in a different world.

You could never understand China. No-one can. Its complexity baffles all super computers. What seems modern can be ancient. Chinese live in their history. They know the Emperors, plots and issues from the past. They never forget. Our Western History to them is just yesterday. The last Emperor of the Qing Dynasty left a couple of hours ago.

Change in the last Century has been constant. But this does not indicate a change in Society. Whatever changes Chairman Mao made have been reformed again. The result is a strange combination of Capitalism, Socialism and Feudalism all meshed in a complex society.

Amazing is not a good enough word to describe this place. It is the be-all and end-all of social laboratories.

New concepts and technology are mixing with ancient practices. China is in space and second and third wives are back with a vengeance. The most kind-hearted people living together with some of the cruellest you will ever see. Contradictions are everywhere.

The journey to China, for many, takes the form of a Train Ride from Hong Kong to Lo Wu on the border with Shenzhen.

Sheung Shui

He got off the Train at the last stop, and Sheung Shui, instead, to say good-bye briefly to Hong Kong. He always did this. Sheung Shui was all farms over thirty years ago, a military buffer area between China and British Hong Kong. Now it was a bustling city of four hundred thousand, the last major stop before China, and where Shenzhen and Hong Kong merge. Cheaper housing and government resettlement estates made this town boom. Sheung Shui is not upscale Hong Kong but it is the real heart of Hong Kong.

If you ever want to learn about Hong Kong, go here at 7am. This is the real Hong Kong. People are rushing to work, tired but moving fast. They need to get there. Students are going to their schools, not really rushing. Hawkers are selling Chinese delicacies like fish balls and buns. Small time couriers are loading their bags for the trip across the border. Filipino maids take care of the elderly in small parks underneath a fierce sun that makes your hair burn. It is the rush of the Hong Kong morning.

It is a morning scene that has been going on for decades. It is the daily renewal of the dream and hope that made Hong Kong a great city.

The first step in learning again is sometimes just to stop and watch. Learn learn from them. Take that time and you will be repaid. The truth sometimes can only be found at 7am in a small town.

These were his happiest times, too early for problems and so easy to enjoy.

The trip from Sheung Shui to Lo Wu takes about five minutes. You have to cross the Hong Kong Border and then cross the Chinese Border which means two stamps on your passport in one hundred metres. Now the Border is an efficient crossing machine. Sometimes Lo Wu handles over two hundred thousand people in one day. The Hong Kong side is notoriously slower than the Chinese side.

This is such a transformation from the one lane railroad bridge before the opening of China. In the past several years more border crossings have been created, and now things are much smoother than before. Lo Wu is still the old stand-by for all Chinese borders and really part of history.

Lo Wu Cemetery

He had one more stop to make. Walking to the end of the Shenzhen Customs entrance, he glanced up back towards the Hong Kong side of the border. This is another must see. Maybe the must see of all must sees. On the hillside behind the border is a very large graveyard. At night you can see many candles burning, which gives the hill a reddish hue.

Hundreds of lights on the last hill before China.

The graves face China, and are the last resting place of a generation that could not return. These people and families chose, with special permission, to be buried at the closest point to China so as to be closer to their past lives and loved ones.

It is the most romantic gesture and the most beautiful place in both Hong Kong and Shenzhen, maybe all of China. There may be no other place like it. For them it meant everything to be close to the China of their youths, to have their bones face home.

Lu Wu Graveyard is more than patriotism. It signifies undying love for China and family, and a desire for proximity that politics had made impossible. It was a separation they would not tolerate; so powerful was this desire to be close to their homeland. He always made a point to bow to these, whose final resting place was of love itself, love for homeland and love for a past before a better today.

They were special people and the symbolism was sometimes more than he could imagine. If you want to understand the Chinese at their most precious level, go to Lo Wu Cemetery. This is what China is and always will be. Love itself.

Mainland China is still about home. The rush of millions to get back to home and family at Chinese New Year is a yearly event, the greatest yearly movement of people in the World. Home and Family are central to all

Chinese, wherever they may be. Home and Family are what makes their hearts beat and what gives them purpose in life. Six thousand years has given them a strong instinct that has not been destroyed by modern ways.

A tear always came with the deepest respect when he saw this cemetery. It just said it all. He could never go to Lo Wu without remembering those departed and buried there, and viewing the last hill before China. It was a good send-off before entering Shenzhen, and the new China.

But one last look at Hong Kong.

A reverse look.

Every Morning Thousands of Hong Kong Chinese make their way back to Hong Kong after spending their nights in Shenzhen. You will only see this in the early morning and late at night.

They are Hong Kong'sKong's blue collar exiles. Forced out by the cost of living, they live on the other side of the border. Leaving early to work and arriving late at night. They have literally been priced out of Hong Kong. Their low salaries keep them away from the place they love.

Some bought apartments in Shenzhen. These are the citizens of Hong Kong ignored by the gleaming towers and Mercedes Benzes that you see. They are economic refugees, moving down the class spectrum. It is a reverse exodus that is rarely noted. So many common workers can survive only in Shenzhen. Hong Kong is no longer their home.

Shenzhen

Turning toward China, he was now in Shenzhen. Back Home to his Glorious Exile.

Shenzhen was growing every day. Everyday it was larger and seemingly richer. Shenzhen was the apogee of Chinese Capitalism. A twenty-five year old city of fourteen million, it was bigger than any city in the United States.

With an inner ring of successful companies and an outer ring of low-end factory towns, Shenzhen was the marvel of the last twenty years. New Cars shared the road with food vendors on the sidewalks pushing tricycles and selling pirated DVDs. Young college students rushing for their first jobs, along with long lines of graduates desperate for that job. A busy city. Not a happy city.

China had much to be proud of. Never before had so many people risen from poverty in the history of the world.

Never before.

Never before had such a huge middle-class appeared. Apartments were selling for over two thousand dollars a square metre. Car sales were booming. Chinese were taking their first vacations all over the world. Gleaming new office towers rise from the border symbolizing a New China.

All of this from nothing.

Thirty years ago, where this great new city stood, there were farms. This was the fastest and most rambunctious growth ever. To see it and think about what had happened should take your breath away.

New Airports dotted the country. Toll roads and magnificent new apartments lined the boulevards. It was Hong Kong again in terms of growth, but at a scale of development beyond imagination. The area alone had over one hundred miles long and sixty miles wide of factories.

The province of Guangdong itself had a population bigger than Mexico. This was the greatest industrial base that the world had ever seen.

An incredible effort and—without exaggeration—the greatest man-made economic transformation ever.

What do you say when you see something like this? There were not even words to express the magnitude of the effort. This effort on the part of the Chinese people was bigger than splitting the atom or going to the moon or winning a hundred gold medals. To be in and around it was perhaps to miss exactly what was before your eyes. It verged on Super Human. It needed to be recognized and recorded in the *Guinness Book of Records* and enshrined in the Wonders of the World. It was just simply that incredible.

To imagine the fierce daily labour of millions of people working earnestly every day to transform a nation within twenty years was probably impossible. What we take for fact was indeed a miracle.

He could not spend one minute in China without wanting to praise such a race; to marvel at their dedication and their ability to change to limits without precedent.

No-one had ever changed so fast and completely. He loved them for this and so much. They were his people. So much feeling pent up inside, so much ability. When they had a dream they would go all out and that was all there was. When they believed in something they could move mountains. When they believed....

This was not forced labour. This was the willing massive migration of over three hundred million souls all trying for the same goal. The goal was to work hard, improve your lot and take care of your family. This was the basic root of this amazing miracle.

Yes, it was a goal of materialism. It was the greatest desire to have more, and live comfortably from the labour of your years. It was the American Dream, the Industrial Revolution, and all that we had ever striven for on the planet for the last five hundred years, all encompassed in one great motion by one nation in one snapshot of time.

It was an undertaking so immense that we perhaps will never be able to record it.

That is, as long as it continues.

But whether it continues or not, it will remain forever the greatest wonder of the world.

The greatest accomplishment in human history.

Chairman Mao said it all on 1 October 1949, the day he declared, "China has stood up"!

But that was not the question.

The question was, Had China woken up? Standing up and waking up are different things.

Reality Check

Number Seven was calling to ask where he was. Where was the money? The situation with her father was getting desperate. What was he doing?

One really had to live in two worlds. What you saw and heard, and what you knew. He could no more escape this reality than the Chinese could escape the fact that only ninety-nine years ago there was an Emperor in Beijing. China, for all its accomplishments, was still a cruel country. Yes, life was cruel anywhere. But walking along the rows of storefront massage parlors with six to eight girls inside—all in debt to the Mafia—could bring any great accomplishment into a different light.

His great love, #7, was in a bind. Since the new modern wonder of the world, China, had no real health insurance and families were smaller now, the burden of taking care of their families falls on the one or two children the government now allows in a family.

His great love had a father to take care of, and not enough money to do it. Since she was not one of the educated few, she could go work as prostitute, or hope for a rich husband. A normal wage would not save her father. And Chinese care about their families more than anything. This was not wonder-of-the-world stuff. You would not see it, or hear it.

It was reality for so many here. You might as well be in El Salvador. The great economic boom had lifted up many, but left many with financial pressures that bordered on unbearable. Yes, a classic third-world economic situation, but with dramatic twists that could shake the whole world.

He believed there was only a short time1200 days left before it all came crashing down.

Outside of the rich factory owners and Government officials and educated élite, the country was in trauma. The wages paid were not keeping up with inflation. Workers could go shopping but buy nothing. The dream was dying an agonized death. University graduates were not finding jobs that paid enough to meet their great responsibilities. There was unrest all over the country, but most of all there was unrest in their hearts. A Chinese cannot accept inequality. This is a rare trait. But each one wants to be the boss. —Why does he have it all and I have nothing? Why has it all slowed down?

Success stories were getting rarer. Those who had money had money, but those born later were not doing so well. Everyday there was more pressure from the family. An Uncle was sick. The new clothes store had no business. This was the silence that was going to destroy the country.

The Olympics were costing forty billion dollars and the people knew in their hearts that it was all for nothing. The sound of the cracking was almost impossible to hear but the scars were seen everywhere. You just had to feel the wind and look at their faces. Hope was gone.

The pride in great accomplishment was wilting under a billion pressures that were building up everywhere. No-one could admit the failure. — What failure? They We had accomplished so much.

Yet it was there and every day the great purpose that had started the venture slowed down under the weight of future failure. It was going to be bad so soon.

It was more than a stock market based on false financial reports. It was what happens when you forget the people completely. When the new TV and wealth never imagined makes you forget everything but yourself. It was a let them eat cake situation. No Social Structure can develop No Social Structure. There was no safety-net. Our World itself had no safety-net.

They had gone too far to see the critical error that was going to explode in the near future. The pressure was building beyond words. Time was running out.

What you could do in a small city-state like Hong Kong or Singapore could never be replicated in a huge country like China or Indonesia or India for that matter. It was not about pollution or industry. It was just the fact that we had all forgotten about each other.

And all this could end so soon.1200 days before the End. Strikes and Riots could would break out all over the country. The workers could not make enough to live and inequality had reached its zenith. The victims would be the Rich and Middle-Class and the Government. The pressure cooker was going to explode.

China would be the greatest victim. There would be burned cars and smoke in the streets. Local Governments would be destroyed by twenty-five years of pent up anger and perceived injustice. There would be Emergency messages and troops on the streets, while everyone with money was trying to flee. CNN would be broadcasting the fall of the Chinese Government. That was the future, unless something changed soon.

This was a world-wide problem. China was going to pay a great price for a disease that had infected all of us. It was just not acceptable to have less. We all needed need eight pairs of shoes and two cars. We need to keep up with the neighbours and get that bit of green.

But corrupt? He had loved to criticize them for corruption. They were no more corrupt than the US government which had failed us completely, or the investment bankers, incapable of analyzing what they had done, while they cashed their bonus cheques.

It was the inequality of a cruel country and the class mentality which was going to destroy them.

Follow the Leader. What we were seeing from Washington made Beijing, New Delhi, Moscow and Cairo now seem pristine. That was sad.

Again, we were being exposed as much worse than the rest.

But we would get off with just a slap on the wrist again. We could just clean the house. They would struggle and be shot. While the world burned, we would be watching the Steelers beat the Browns one more time and Manchester United play Bayern Münich again and again. .

We all needed to realize that enough had to be enough or the planet would only get worse. We sold them our ever growing capitalism. We sold them hard work makes all right. But never spoke about our own greed and unhappiness. TheirThere mistake was to believe too strongly. Our mistake was to be so cynical.

Yes, it is important to take care of each other.

Yes, it is important to be content with less.

World Business traveler be damned!

This was a change even Obama could not understand. It was change so profound that unfortunately only more suffering could bring it about. We had to care more for each other and even the damn playing field. There is no Super-Bowl. There are no champions.

We all really needed just to raise the white flag and drop to our knees. It was time to be someone and something else. We had evolved and gone the wrong way. There were no more soldiers and no more gold in the treasury for the incredible mistakes we had been making. We had screwed up and needed to admit it.

What an amazing turn around! Call it an Act of God. Call in AIG, they will cover it. No more excuses. The System was doomed. It was sad but true. It was a fact.

His driver was waiting for him in a nearby parking lot. Ah Peng. If he could, he would be at his side always or at least until each other's hair had gone grey. Ah Peng. Everyone should have a friend/assistant like this.

Driving all day in ninety degree heat was tough. Ah Peng could find a factory in the middle of this industrial wasteland like no other. He drove in a calm and dignified fashion at all times. Ah Peng would adjust the volume of his CDs and feed his Dog when he was travelling and get him cigarettes, pick up his dry-cleaning and get him sleeping pills if he could not sleep.

This was the kind of person that had built up this new China. He lived within his means; no mahjong; no card playing; no gambling. Except for the occasional drinking bouts, where the alcohol was still there in the morning he was a tolerant respectful man. But who was he to talk about drinking bouts anyway? Ah Peng's salary was more than average, but he deserved more.

Trust and friendship were funny things here. There was really only a little of each. Your best friend would betray you if given the chance. He knew so many people and had so few friends. Though it would be wrong to say no-one helped him. This he got all the time. Being a foreigner in a Chinese world you got away with a lot of things that others would not. You did not suffer the penalties. The truth was they treated you very well.

Getting close was much tougher. You were different and people stared at you. Even though he spoke great Chinese and knew so much, he would probably never get past the business façade or the ""This is how we talk" to foreigners" routine.

The Chinese knew he was different and treated him differently but "close" was not a word he would use. No-one was really close to anyone. But at least he could say he was as close as you could get, and understood more than other foreigners did. Or even better and most importantly, they knew he could feel them and the pressure of their lives. This was his key skill and was worth a lot.

He was also becoming a Chinese and that meant a lot. It meant that for him, just like for them, life was a heavy thing and each month seemed like a year. It meant there was never a moment of real peace. It meant his mind was never at rest.

To say that Chinese think all the time is an understatement. They are always thinking. The CPU does not turn off. They do not just sit and day-dream. They are always thinking about their problems or how to deal with someone or a situation. They don'tdon't just sit and stare at a wall. They think constantly. It is both amazing and frightening. Six thousand years of civilization have created a billion thinkers and calculators.

We in the West are much more bent towards mystic thinking. We are easily pleased and complacent. The Chinese mind is not. They focus intensely on each situation and keeping up with them was both his greatest pleasure and greatest challenge.

To live in China is to be constantly playing chess with each and every situation and every comment has a direction. Yes. Machiavelli would have been right at home here. But having to guess and second-guess every moment is both exhilarating and tiresome. China is like that. Complex to the fifteenth degree and multiply that by one and a half billion and nothing can compare.

Ah Peng was thinking of what to say. Scratching his head slowly he asked..", "Are we going to the Apartment or the Office."?"

"No, we need to go the Baoan Keyboard Factory. I need to see Boss Wang."

A strange look crossed Ah Peng's face. This was not the expected answer or his usual. Off they went.

The trip would take about forty-five minutes through miles and miles of factories. Driving through the depths of Shenzhen is an experience. Smoke, thousands of trucks, traffic jams with people crossing the highway and bags of cement falling to the ground gave Ah Peng a daily challenge as they navigated through a bustling city.

It was a modern desert of grey buildings and clothes hanging out of windows, where eight workers slept every night. The Bright Sun made it look so cruel and so heartless.

The economy was getting worse. There were more people on the street doing nothing. Unemployment in China was over fifty percent. You never saw anyone over forty working except in the most menial of jobs. Factories were starting to close.

It was so far a silent menace. The unemployed were back in the provinces, not doing much of anything. Their children were here in the wasteland working in factories, responsible for everything. There was a growing sense of purposelessness at the bus-stops. There were more blank stares. Another day of crossing the city in the endless heat looking for a new job was beyond exhausting.

The feeling was not one of triumph but one of despair. Sundays were especially marked as the workers went out, entered the stores and bought nothing. Money was short. You simply could not live on the salary or buy meat for that matter. It was heart-rending to know and to feel. And it was more heart-rending to feel so much and never show it. But the pain was growing and getting harder to bear every day. He could feel the despair in the air. They would never show it on their faces.

Red Guards with Cadillacs

Boss Wang's factory was on a nondescript street in just another one of the factory ghettoes. Forgotten. With quite a bit trash all over the street.

This was not Beijing. This was where the poor lived and worked. All but forgotten by everyone, except when we get a great deal on the new DVD player or an IPOD that we have been waiting to buy. It was here on this dirty street that all we buy was made.

The price of our system.

Fifteen to eighteen-year olds starting their life like Charles Dickens in twelve to eighteen-hour shifts, while we watched *Survivor* and forgot everything.

He was as guilty as anyone. Perhaps more, because he knew what the price was and how much would be paid later for that new set of golf-clubs and designer-shirts.

The growling security guard let the car in without much of a growl.

And it was a surprise move. He had to try to put some new orders in with the Factory and get them all ready so that he could later ambush them with the Eric issue. Like a Chinese opera, the plot had to move real slow, and with a lot of facial movements, so that the trap could be sprung at a later time. If there was no opera there would be no resolution to anything.

Being direct and honest always meant defeat. If you were going to be direct it had to be for a reason. Each movement needed to be planned out in advance. It was Chinese rules of war here. Being unpredictable was always the best. Never act the same. Stay on story. Be an Actor. These were Chinese rules. Never show your true intent.

While Chinese are famous for being cold and calculating, get them mad and they explode. This had been his undoing many times. Sometimes it was the cold simmering anger of revenge. Sometimes it was a tidal wave of emotion and tears. Sometimes it was a look and departure forever with the cell-phone dead to the world. He had probably experienced every nuance of their anger by now in his life. It was easy to recognize, and much harder to avoid. He was a very slow but very thorough learner. A month without incident was a record.

The Monkey loved to cause a ruckus.

His first move today was to go to visit the boss of the factory, Mr Wang.

Mr WangWu was in his fifties and a former Red Guard of the Cultural Revolution. Who knew what events he and every Chinese over the age of forty-five had witnessed in those days? Obviously none of this had hurt him. In fact he had once said that, when he thought back to his Red Guard Days, they were good memories.

This was a real touchy subject. Depending on which side you sat on, you either looked at this time as wonderful or the worst thing that ever happened.

He was from the North. Each area of China had its own business-style. Northerners were more direct. Bosses from Hubei were famous for lying. Bosses from Guangdong could be your friends. Bosses from Sichuan were undependable and Bosses from Ningpo were the smartest of all. Shanghai, well, that was another Hong Kong. They even now had Filipino maids and English-speaking children to go along with them on vacations to Hainan. They could do anything.

Speaking of the Red Guards, where were all those millions of screaming and Red Book shaking youths? They were here amongst us. Despite the fact that the last thirty years had been a complete repudiation of those times, it was these very people who were in a position to gain the most from Opening and Reform.

Being Party members of loyal standing they got the best Factory positions and no official repudiation was ever made of each and every one of them. Of course, there was the famous Gang of Four trial with Jiang Ching, the wife of

Chairman Mao, being jailed as she denied each and every charge.

But what about the millions of devotees who broke into homes and jailed the counter revolutionaries, who were often nothing but recent government officials and people of influence?

The Cultural Revolution was a second revolution within the Party itself. It was a most bitter period for so many, and yet a period of progress for others. When one Dog falls, another must rise. Today'sToday's landlord was perhaps yesterday's Red Guard.

While this is not what our modern understanding says, it remains essentially true. A huge proportion of today'stoday's successful leaders and business persons come directly from that group. In this complicated world, fortunes were changed forever via this difficult political transformation.

You could be up and then way down in the blink of an eye. Equally you could be down and raised up in the most trivial of circumstances. This is essentially the story of the past sixty years, a long chain of rising and falling. This was life in China.

When the dice were rolled you ended up in your current situation. What does the factory worker think when he sees Boss WangWu drive out in his Cadillac? He thinks…", "There is no difference between us, other than your situation twenty years ago and my family'sfamily's misfortune. I could be the Boss but your situation was better. That is all. You do not deserve it.".'' And those are very scary thoughts. The hate and dislocation brought on by those years is still alive in all.

There is no meritocracy at all. No-one deserves anything in the eyes of anyone else. Boss WangWu knows it and so does everyone else.

Thus we have a double edged sword. The Rich are no more secure than the poor. If this could happen once, it could happen again and there is no way to bridge this gap.

Hearts are filled with this type of thinking. This is not California or the United States where all are equal in the Super Market. This was not socialism any more.

This is a very deeply ingrained thinking that pervades even the most humble of workers. This is what remains of class struggle covered up by fancy TV shows and Nationalism. Each and every one has a position. This can be seen by their clothes, the car they drive. And each strives to increase this position over time. You can tell someone'ssomeone's economic status by just looking at the clothes they wear. But you need to look closely.

As Chairman Mao would say, this was just a continuation of class struggle. No-one wants to hear this, but position and place have replaced the Comrades, and social ranks have come back. Ninety-nine years is all we have between us and the Emperor himself.

The Big Four are a car, house, English and a Foreign Education. This is great status for anyone. If you have achieved these, you can walk down the street or drive down the road with your head held high above everyone else. If you have these you can strut into the hotel like ArthurRichard, and let everyone see your status.

Of course, the more the better.

The new advertisement for the Mercedes C Class shows others watching in awe and the joys of passing a bicycle rider.

Forget the people. I am ahead of you.

It was as if all anyone cared about in all of Asia was making money. The West had won.

Six thousand five hundred years of culture was now absorbed in an endless and fruitless pursuit of money. All that was spiritual was washed in a bath of venom and destroyed. What was left was the feeling of emptiness. There were no great thinkers left in the country and calculators had taken the place of philosophy and social ethics. The last gaspgrasp was the call for Social Harmony.

The great reawakening seemed both so far away and yet so close. The Mirage was just beginning to turn into a nightmare. Reality was absorbed by a dark and confusing cloud.

Instead of learning from them, they were learning from us. And not learning anything that in the long run would be good. You could hardly blame them. We applauded each and every mistake and called it Progress and a Step toward Westernization and Democracy.

We cheered each and every opening of a new Corporate Headquarters and never saw the tears in a far away village or the pain of departure as young men and women took the three or four day bus trip to the city to work in the factory.

China would soon wake up. Somebody call the fire brigade, quickly!

Luckily Boss WangWu was in. He could tell by the Golden Cadillac parked in the awning by the Factory wall. The inner security officers let him in without question. He had to climb up four floors to get to the Office.

Greeting him was Ms Vicky, the head of sales to foreigners. Her surprise was evident. Like in most of the companies, foreign sales are handled by an English-speaking College Graduate.

"   "Oh, Monkey King! What a surprise."

"I am here to see Boss Wang."

"Great! He will be glad to see you."."

The first rule was always only talk to the Boss. The Sales person was not in charge of anything. Making about four hundred to six hundred dollars a month and educated, she was designated to deal with foreigners and that was all. She did not handle pricing or anything. She was the screen in front of the Boss.

This was the Chinese way. Her power came from her ability to communicate with the Foreign Devils. This was the best job she could get. Not the job she dreamed of.

She was working in a dreary factory for a boss she despised.

There was hate in her eyes and in the eyes of all the workers. This was not a good or happy factory. Maybe they were badly paid or maybe they were sick of seeing a Golden Cadillac in the Boss'sBoss's parking lot.

Vicky'sVicky's pay level was way below what she expected after studying long and hard. She was the hope of her family in a far away province and had to tolerate this strange deviation to her dreams. Buying an apartment was impossible, but she would persevere in the hope that somehow her situation would improve.

Entering Boss Wang's office, he saw a local police officer sitting on the leather couch and drinking tea. Boss WangWu was surprised to see him and probably suspicious of the visit.

""Monkey King, Comrade, come on in!"

"Thanks, Comrade! I was just at the airport back from the US. I want you guys to get working on some orders.".".

The Police Officer was duly impressed by the Foreigner speaking fluent Chinese.

Boss WangWu was also happy to hear about his prosperity but even more happy to show the Police Officer his good fortune.

"   "The Monkey King is a very good customer of ours. He is just like a Chinese now.".".

The police officer smiled and nodded. He was both embarrassed and realizing that whatever business he was trying to conduct with Boss WangWu had been interrupted. It would have to wait for another day. Boss WangWu was now delighted. He could get rid of the Police Visit, which was probably for no good, and show off his contact with the Foreigners at the same time. The Police Officer got up to leave. The meeting was finished. He could not continue with a Foreigner in the room. A short good-bye and he was gone. Mission accomplished.

Boss WangWu smiled. Yes, this was going to be one of those Chinese-puzzle conversations.

" "You should thank me, Boss Wang.Wu. I got the Police guy to leave you alone."

"No problem, Monkey King. No problem. You are our very important customer."

"Well, that is good news. Because I have some new orders. Let me see the new model of the multimedia keyboard that you told me about last month."

"Sure. I thought you said it was too expensive?"

"I just got back from a meeting in the US and that may be just what they want."

A quick call to Vicky, who came in with the sample as Boss WangWu poured some of his special tea in a tiny cup. He would make sure that you could see it was over five hundred dollars a pound, by rumpling the tea container and with an obvious twist showing you the name on the box. This tea was Pu Erhh, the tea of the rich and famous. The rage of tea-drinkers all over China.

It was said it would only get better with time. People were buying it as an investment. Boss WangWu was going out of his way to make the Monkey King feel his blessing and give and show face. This was not offered to the Policeman who had just left and even Vicky while handing the sample keyboard to him noticed. She would not be offered this tea either. The compliment was noticed and appreciated. Vicky quickly left.

""Incredible Tea, Boss WangWu, I have never had this before."."

This was not true. All the Bosses were drinking this tea now.

""Oh, nothing. I just got it when I went to Yunnan last month. So, what do you think about the keyboard? Just finished the mould."

"It'sIt's really nice. You said it was how much? Three dollars fifty?""

Boss WangWu smiled.

""I don'tdon't remember. Maybe a bit higher now. The US Dollar is falling, you know."

"Yes, I know. Sorry about that. The world economy is bad. I noticed you did not have so many orders as before?"?"

Boss WangWu, smiled again.

""Business is OK. But I have to pay the workers more and more. So yes, it is harder.".."

The final point had been reached. Even with his huge apartment and Cadillac, Boss WangWu needed the business. Who knew what kind of problems he had. Loans from Banks? Problems with the Police?

""Boss WangWu, I have several container orders. So I need a good price. Please have Vicky send me your best price today via email. Then, I can check with the customer. Please give me this sample, so I can send it for approval. OK?"

"Of course, Monkey King. Vicky will send the pricing later."

"I need it today, OK?"

"Yes, sure. No Problem, Monkey King. Everything for you." ."

He had to ask, and knew that the price would not be ready until he had called three times or more, and may be not for one day or two. This was another part of the play, not an inefficiency.

Boss WangWu could not show he wanted the business and he could not let on that he wanted it badly. Vicky would send it only when the Boss said to. It would not be today.

"Monkey King, do you want to go out drinking tonight? The Girls just love you and you just love the Girls. How about it?"

"Sorry, Boss. I still have another factory to go to. The customer wants two samples. Let'sLet's go next week. What great tea!. I thank you. Need to hurry now. One more meeting on this".."

Now the price would be ready sooner. If there was competition, things would go faster. With a smile and bow, he left. He smiled at Vicky and asked her to make sure to send the price. She smiled and said, "No problem!" He would have his Assistant call tomorrow. Then maybe the first act of the Opera would be rolling, but there might be more. The score was not written yet. Boss WangWu would think this one through for longer.

Getting back in the car with Ah Peng, he felt bad.

But there was no other way.

The Factory had given him bad products. Really the thinking was, "We are not making much money any way, so why care?"

This is what he saw every day. Factories were in trouble and this was percolating down through the whole organization. Where there had once been a rush, now there was just no interest in anything. You almost felt bad asking anyone to do anything, because no-one was getting ahead anyway. The battle was being lost.

The Spirit of Capitalism was quietly drowning. There was no escape from this lie. None of us could escape the same feeling. It was not up, up, and away. It was a slow deflation and the loss of confidence. Fireworks and Olympics and Space Missions were the best the Emperor could give. What was next? Gladiators, maybe, when Survivor and The Apprentice failed us. We had lost that loving feeling. We were eating our young and enjoying it.

The theme for the Olympics in China was right on.

"One World, One Dream."

This was really the crux of the issue. When there is a dream, people can do anything.—Americans, Chinese, Germans, Russians.—All of us can do anything, when we believe. We can fall in love, be inventive, or destructive, but we must believe. When the belief dies, we live in an era of cynics and fools. The Chinese were losing the feeling now. The rest of the World was also. Take the Dream away, and you lose it all.

Caleb Kavon, The Monkey in Me

America's Got Talent and The Bone. My Ass.

Three Tigers

The next stop was even further away. They were going to another factory to load a container of speakers for Mexico.

This was going to be nice, because he could see the Three Tigers, the owners of the factory. They were called the Three Tigers because they were all born in the year of the Tiger. One was born in 1950, the next in 1962, and third was born in 1974.

The Tiger is both tenacious and capable and always worthy of respect. Each Chinese Year is different. 1950 was the year of the Golden Tiger. 1962 was the year of the Water Tiger and 1974 was the year of the Wooden Tiger. Each Tiger had different skills and abilities. To be with 3three Tigers was both interesting, rare, and daunting.

Mr Hu, the oldest and Golden Tiger of the Group, was amazingly gentle and helpful. He was cultured, persuasive and educated. In addition to being a Golden Tiger, he represented the first children of the Chinese Revolution. He had seen the transformation of China, from Famine in the early 1960s to the Cultural Revolution and to the Great Opening of which we all were part. He knew what Chairman Mao said when Lin Biao disappeared in a crashed plane in Mongolia. He had seen Deng Xiao Ping on his tour of Guangdong and the South in the 1980s that resulted in the Opening. He could remember all the changes in the system and in people over the decades.

A former Party member, Hu was both amazing and intelligent.

""Oh it'sit's the Monkey King. You were right, the economy is crashing. How did you know?"

"I just study Chairman Mao, Comrade. Too many contradictions. People driving Mercedes and Bicycles on the same street causes resentment and you cannot have such a big gap in wealth."

"Monkey King, don'tdon't you think that the Americans have caused this?"

"Yes, we all have. We cannot live like this any more. We should have learned from China in the 1970s. But China learned from us and none of it is good. The Americans have acted like fools, but China has been just as bad by allowing this brutal version of capitalism to be created. The people did not benefit from all of this—only a small portion of them who live far above the masses."

The Golden Tiger stopped to think.

"Comrade Hu, they contradicted all that was taught in your youth. Now China is part of the system and people cannot eat meat. Don'tDon't worry about the Americans, they have everything. I am worried about China now."

"You might be right.—I am worried, our business is terrible.".""

As he was speaking, Mr Tan, the Water Tiger, came in. The Water Tiger is practical and goal-oriented. Mr Tan was born in 1962, the year of the great man-made famine that struck China from 1959 to 1962. He had known both great poverty and great wealth in his life. He was worried also.

""Well, Monkey, you were right. Our business is bad. Not sure what to do now."

"Mr Tan, firstly don'tdon't move to the new factory. Stay here in the old Factory. You should not expand now, business is getting harder."

"Yes, we should think about it.".""

The Third Tiger was Mr Liu.. He was in charge of sales and the junior partner in the venture. He had only known success and had never seen anything but constant growth. He represented the modern and educated China. China was going to be a super-power, China was in Space, China was #1 in the Olympics.

""Monkey King, You don'tdon't think the Olympics was a good thing?"

"Not if children cannot go to school and the factory workers are suffering. Gold medals mean nothing."

"But all America does is fight overseas. Look at Vietnam and Iraq. It is crazy."

"Yes, that is true. They cannot fight these wars for long. They are broken. It makes me sad for all of us. All will suffer for these crimes. The Wealth Gap is just too large."

"What will we do? We aren'taren't making much money and it is hard to pay the workers more."

"China has always been here. It will always be here. You have done more than any country to change. You should all be proud. But there will be more changes. We all need to change. It will be easier for the Chinese to change their mentality than for the Americans. They will have to adjust very quickly. But China couldwill have strikes all over the country. It could get ugly. But you are my friends, and yes, I have more orders for you next week. Let'sLet's slowly make the change. Try to remember all that is good in our lives and we can care for each other through this hard time. Remember all people are one family. These are the words of Jesus and China is the People'sPeople's Republic of China." ."

All of the Tigers sat quietly and drinking tea.

The Three Tigers were all good men. Not cruel. They were reasonable and good businessmen. He would always continue to support them.

They were the China that he loved. They did not drive Golden Cadillacs and were humble in manners, management and clothes. They did not over-spend or show off. Their workers worked in peace and as friends. There was none of the hate that he felt in the Factory of Boss Wang.Wu.

The 3Three Tigers would prevail. They would be the ones to put reason back in the world when the problems came to a head. They were the new China that would soon be born. He loved them and their style. With them China had hope; and with Boss WangWu, China would be finished. It would be a struggle and the Third Revolution since the Emperor had been forced out.

They were happy with the new orders and spent the next forty minutes watching the workers load the container out of the warehouse. He did some inspection and testing of the products. All was fine. If you cannot trust Three Tigers, who can you trust?

Ah Peng drove him through the factories back home. The night was rising like a Dragon through the Red Ball of the falling Sun.

Highways are so impersonal. Never close to another car. Rushing. Driving Fast. Even this was a loss. Stoplights were needed everywhere. So we could see each other again. Side by Side. It was not what we wanted. It was what we had to have.

The night was: Construction workers sitting down to eat in front of the work site. Lights going on in the apartments. Factory workers finally getting off work. Headlights and bright neon advertisements. Noodle Shops and Bicycles. He could look out of the window on the miracle of life itself.—Obscured by the dark he could see and be part of it. The Night was back.

He called #7. Her phone was turned off again. He sighed, loud enough for Ah Peng to hear.

""Boss, are you OK?"

"Fine, Ah Peng. Just tired. The plane trip was very tiring."

"It must be. You came back from such a distant place, as far as the Moon."

"You are right. I feel like I am back from the Moon or may be I am still there?"?"

They drove in silence as the night time rush was ending. Ah Peng took him to his small apartment. He would go to the main office tomorrow, he hoped.

""Ah Peng, thank you. Tomorrow, get me more of those sleeping-pills. I still am not sleeping well."

"Sure, Boss. I will pick you up at 10am…"."

Reflections on Dark Clouds during the New Moon

The apartment was nothing special. And it was no longer a home. It was here that his drama with #7 had been played. It was here that he was almost always in the no-man'sman's land of his soul.

He was not sure that the place had any good memories. They had been having problems basically since the Chinese New Year. He had never felt important. She would just not say what was on her mind. He had no idea what she thought about anything.

It was one of those living together but living separately situations. He would call her and she would not answer. He had never figured her out and she probably did not want to figure him out. He could not totally blame her. His life was not all that exciting. She hated his drinking. He hated her silence. They were not a team. Each person had his/her own agenda. Each wanted to run the show. He wanted more from her. She either did not have it to give or simply would not.

There had been some fights. They would fight; she would leave and not come back for several days. Then she would return with a remorseful look. He was so glad to see her that he never wanted to talk about the problems that had caused the fight in the first place.

She had been gone for 7seven weeks now. He was getting used to the pain, a dull ache that never went away. Like duelling dragons their life together was a constant circling. He would rise one day, she the next. It was the mating of snakes or of wild horses, but without passion. One bite here, another there. Two people that no-one could live with—trying to live together.

For two weeks after her departure he had looked out of the window desperately trying to find her. Was that her down there? Maybe it was her coming back. It was brutal and confusing.

One Day—during a rainstorm, while on the street— he thought he saw her through the foggy glass of a passing taxi. He was never sure. Maybe it was her, maybe not.. Nevertheless, he kept looking. He was looking for a Ghost, and looking for something to return that had never been there.

What was it? Maybe this.

She was silent. He never knew what was on her mind. He was insistent, you had to know his every thought, or he would force it on you. She wanted peace and silence. He wanted war and struggle. She wanted him to trust and understand her. He only wanted to be understood. She understood him. He would not understand her.

She wanted to breathe. He would not let her. He was selfish, and she was independent. It was the Scorpion losing to Sagittarius. He was weak and she was strong. His anger simmered over every slight. Her pride was wounded. His pride was without its expected revenge.

Just being here was a punishment.

He had said some words and she had left with her phone turned off. He had said too much. She had reacted too strongly. He had changed the locks. She had returned and could not get in. She had disappeared. He threw away half of her clothes, but could not throw them all away. He had called her turned-off cell-phone a thousand times and stopped eating. He could not get her out of his mind. One second he was hating and rejecting her forever, the next screaming for her company. It was torture not knowing where she was or what had happened.

Her absence did not make his heart grow fonder. It made him more bitter by the day. He did not think this could work, but could not dissipate the need he felt for her. She could never give him the love and sustenance he needed, but she was the One.

The irony of the situation was beyond obvious. It had been a failure, was a failure and would be a failure. But he did not want any one else. Like a love-stricken sixteen-year old, he was on the verge of emotional collapse. The days passed, and his bad mood and suffering only increased. He could not liberate himself from her, no matter how hard he tried.

Love was like an old CD. Though you might not hear the song any more, it was there. You could push forward to the next song, but the old song was always there. The song of all his loves' loves was there forever. They would never die. You might not hear their song any more but it could never disappear entirely.

Day after Day, he was in pain.

Then one day, after about a month, she had called. She was back in her province, her father was very sick and she needed his help. She did not back down, telling him that she was telling the truth and needed some money. He chastised her for disappearing. She asked his forgiveness and promised that all would go well when her father was better. She asked him why he never trusted her and always said the most hurtful things? He asked her why she never made him feel like he was important to her, which is what he felt everyday in her presence. He asked why she never asked how he was feeling. She asked him why he did not understand the pressure she felt with her sick father and how nervous she always was with this situation. He asked again why he felt she gave him no emotional support. Why did she never answer the phone? And the impasse remained in a stagnant pool, only now with the chance she might return.

At first he was overjoyed. But then fearful. He was not sure how it would work. She probably felt the same. Maybe he was better off without her. She probably felt the same.

He did not in his heart expect her to return.

What had once been so natural was now a Cold War. One more incident and it would be another repetition. He the same, he could not feel any security any more. She had left him just as his mother had done when he was a child.

He was not adult enough to deal with this. She was the adult. He was the child. He did not have her strength, nor her haunting beautiful tragedy. He was suffering for nothing. She was suffering for something. Somehow one did not equal the other. She was his superior in so many ways. How could he manage what he was not big enough to manage? He had never felt so challenged and so not up to the task. He was not big enough for her, too petty, too self engaged. How could you fight a ghost that you could see but not penetrate?

These were the thoughts that had never left him for seven weeks. It was like Napoleon returning from Russia, only to live for Waterloo. One last charge up the hill and the defeat would be total. He had died but had never been reborn. She had died everyday and was looking for the light. He would never give it her.

He doubted he loved her, but said he did. He doubted she loved him as she had never really let him know. What a disaster it was.

He was so full of regret for loving someone he could never know. He was so full of regret for not loving her enough. He was so full of regret that it was totally possible that she did not love him at all and was only using him for money.

Yes, wake up, you fool!

Fooled again.

And again.

Or was he?

You had to give her credit. She could at least stand up to him. In fact she was kicking his Ass in almost every way. She could defend herself. She was tough. No-one walked all over her. He had met his match. He loved the challenge. He loved the fact she was so unpredictable. She kept him guessing and guessing. What was next? Could he trust her? What was going on in her head every night as she sat there and did her needle-point without talking?

Her walking out on him was a new thing. After he had essentially walked out on three marriages, it was quite a shock to be on the receiving end. Though he was much more subtle in his departures, she at least knew how to make a dramatic exit off stage left. He had met his match.

In the end, maybe she was what he needed. Her return was a good sign after such suffering.

He went to the computer and sent her the money. Called her. Her phone was off again. He sent her a text message about the money and that was all. No more, "I love you"s and, "I miss you"s. The Weeks were moving and he could not bring himself to say that again.

And so another night began, he would be burning with the same thoughts from the same angles. The night would end and he would still not have a clue to what was right or wrong.

And so it went every day, the same circle, never reaching a resolution. Here to There and Back. God Help him. His heart knew no peace.

The Desert was all he could see. Barren and Bare.

This, on top of everything. Seven weeks was seven years. He could not shake her. Other women could not do this to him. Misery was his home. Could he break out of this? Thank God he was busy today and could get away from another round of these thoughts.

Or was it this?

In the end, this is what he loved about his life. The constant struggle, the battles never won. He could not live in a tranquil way. He could not be content. He had to have action every day.

Thank You, China.

Land of Bustling Millions…. Bust my chops.

Land of Complexity…. Put me in with the Minotaur. The Monkey King is ready.

Land without Romance. . . . I will open your heart.

He could stay struggling in China'sChina's spider-web forever. Win or lose. China gave him what he needed to live. The constant struggle and uncertainty were manna from Heaven.

He was Joshua waiting for Old Moses at the bottom of Mount Sinai. It was where he was meant to be. He could wait for the Promised Land, and wait forever if necessary. He could endure the desert. He would wait, and be faithful. Moses would eventually come down. He would not be alone forever.

He was the Monkey King always poised for a fight.

It was all a test. A Moon Walk without the giant step for mankind. Like a Samurai jumping off a cliff, he had it all. Everything he had ever wanted he had done. Frank Sinatra, eat your heart out. You don'tdon't need to make it. You need to live. You need to fail. You need to fall in quick-sand. Safe is nothing special.

Be like Mohammed Ali. Box like you don'tdon't care. Show your heart. Change your name. Do the sky-hook. Have them spit on you. Carry the cross. Die and be reborn. Submit to God. Follow the Will of Heaven.

Screw Bear Stearns and Morgan Stanley. We want more.

Bail Out. What a concept.

The US Congress doing a bail-out. This is what you do when your plane is crashing. Bail Out. Run away. Cry. Bail Out. You are failures. Go ahead and Bail Out.

He would not Bail Out of anything.

This had all started after he returned from the war. Though he never had bad war dreams, he never woke up happy. He could not stroll in the woods, smell the flowers. He wanted to wake up and smell the coffee. He could not go into the shopping mall if it was crowded or a busy restaurant. He could not sit too close to someone. His temper would flare up and down. He was not the same kid that had left and wanted to start a band.

He had killed and slept every night with rifle. The look on the face of the dead and maimed stayed with him. It was his scar. He was not ashamed or complaining. It was just how he was now. It was an illness. It was a mild case of classic Post Traumatic Stress.

.   He was not incapacitated but he was affected. Lost marriages and restlessness were partly the result of three years fighting in a far-away land. His youth was given to arms and war. It would never leave him. He was not free any more. He could always hear the bullets and grenades. God Bless America.

And.

Thank You, China.

Thank You, #7, and your six sisters of the past.

Thank You. I love you all. I love you so much that I can'tcan't even think about most of you any more.

He could not change his life. But he came home someone else. He had never known the first person, and the second was someone he was not sure he wanted to know. Too many angles, too many caves, were there in his mind. He wanted to live in the moment and forget the past. Stop defining himself and get on with it. Stop telling the same stories over and over. Get away from the soap opera, and turn off the endless software in his head.

It wasn'twasn't working today. And he took the last of the sleeping pills and very, very slowly went back to sleep.

He woke up after two hours and turned on the International NewsCNN again. Yes there had been a massive bombing in Pakistan at a hotel. Of course, instead of covering this, there was a one hour feature about a hundred-60foot Sailboat sponsored by Qatar Airlines and Rolex or something like that. The owner of the Yacht was a DutchAmerican Real Estate developer. He said he loved the yacht because he liked to organize things.

Looked like a nice guy but he still hoped the Yacht would sink and everyone survive but the Tall Dutch millionaire.

It was the same old story. Why find out what is happening when we can watch a sailboat run by a millionaire? Never start the day solving our problems, but solving our greed, lust, and sense of entitlement.

Why would we want to see the yacht? What relation did this have to anything important in ninety-eight percent of our lives? The world was suffering and we were watching yachts? What blindness. Did these people wake up just like us and open their eyes? Or were their eyes just permanently shut?

Next was a show about international golf. It was some strange story about twin sisters in IndiaIreland who were up and coming on the Golf circuit. Talk about two-headed monsters. The old Werewolf movies were much more interesting.

If God had been more kind we could hear each other'sother's heartbeats. We could walk by and hear the stress in each person'sperson's life. We could hear the happy beating and rapid beating of excitement and fear. We would have some sort of real contact with everyone. But we were both blind and deaf. We needed to hear those hearts all the time. Surely put together it would be the sweetest music in the universe.

He vowed to try.

Still exhausted. It was another night. He had learned to love the hours before the dawn. He would look out of the window and watch China and maybe see #7.

China never sleeps.

At 2am the evening shift workers are getting off and going to eat at the outside food-stands after a long shift. They would slowly go to the stalls, order food and go off into the night. Young couples in love for the first time, singles looking for love and groups of friends and co-workers. Everyone was in the same situation, hoping for a break in life and really hungry for the spicy tofu meat and vegetable barbecue, sometimes mixed with noodles. This was standard late-night fare all over China. He would watch them at intervals until the stalls basically shut down at 4am.

He would watch the trash collectors who appeared at 3.30am. They would check all the garbage for recyclable items and any usable food, moving slowly and pushing bikes. It appeared each one had a street.

At 4.30am the Taxi Drivers would park their vehicles together and sit and play cards together, waiting for things to get busy again at 7am.

At 5am the police vehicle would go for a small breakfast at the same restaurant every day. The first bus would appear at 5.30am with the same people waiting at the stop to start working.

The schedule of life went on with the same consistency as the Big South China Sun would soon rise and bring a rich bright yellow light to the world. Though he was looking out from his balcony, he felt a part of it. The Sun this morning was small, intense and red, with two black slashes caused by the distant clouds.

The Sunrise, instead of inspiring him, just made him more sad and depressed. . Another day to miss his love and another day of defeat in a battle he was not going to win.

The Sun was not his friend. Only the night could give him a measure of peace.

Like an anthropologist he loved to watch everyone, making mental notes of their posture. How they walked and ate and at what time which things happened. It was the nice time of the day. He felt he was with all of them and distant at the same time. He could hear their shoes on the sidewalk, smell the fire of the grill; from his hidden redoubtpoint see them eating, and with them enjoy the short break from a hard day of labour and the promise of deserved rest.

It had become his nightly ritual since #7 left and he could no longer sleep. Everyday he checked the sunrise time so he could go for a walk before the sun came up. He had begun to avoid people unless it was absolutely necessary. He counted the hours until nightfall so as to let another day end and carry him into the beloved dark. This was every day and it was his time. He could work, think and avoid the pain of the day. He wanted to sleep when she was awake, wherever she was.

God, he missed her.

This was clearly why God had made night and day. So we could heal our hearts and rest our souls, before the onset of the Sun made our shortcomings too obvious. This "evil lurks in the heart of night" stuff was not true. The evil was in the day when nothing could hide. Night was peace itself. The monsters walked under the Sun and fled at the onset of darkness.

Night and Sleep were our last refuge, be it from a prison camp, office tower or the crib of an infant. We all deserved a break and deserved one badly. A Cruise Ship was not the answer. Things had to slow down.

All he needed was a beer and a Johnny Cash CD and he would be there.

There'sThere's nothing like a Sunday to make you feel alone.

Yes, he and Johnny Cash were united.

The Man in Black was together in solidarity with the Man in China.

One true love lost and your life was trash. Bolivar was dying friendless at Santa Marta again. The prisoners at Folsom were going back to their cells. Moses was dying without ever getting to the Promised Land. Jose Rizal, the Filipino Hero, was about to die in Luneta Park. The Flags were coming down and not going back up.

But Johnny was lucky in the end,. He had June Carter Cash, to save him. Dick Nixon had Pat Nixon in the years after his resignation. And then again, Samson had

Delilah and Bill deserved Hillary. Elvis had Priscilla and He had nothing. What he really wanted he was not going to get.

At 3am he could check the horoscopes for the next day. He always checked his and of course checked #7's. How pathetic. Checking the horoscope of someone he would not see or hear of or possibly ever know. Trying to get any edge on the cliff that was engulfing him, it all seemed to be so impossible. He had been hurt many times and had no idea why this one meant so much to him.

He always woke up hoping that this was the day he would be over her. Sometimes that feeling would last for a couple of hours and then he was back in the mire of useless thinking.

This probably was not going to work out. He wanted her back and then maybe he never wanted to see her again.

You would think Mankind had already gone through every emotion and action possible over ten thousand years. Some were favourites, like torture and war, and never grew out of style. Others like Art and Good Deeds and High Culture had had their eras. Hate and Love were other constants. Insult and Hurt surely we had tried in every possible combination. Birth and Death we should have had down pat by now, those were standards.

Working and Sharing our Knowledge should be completely under control. After so many generations we should have learnt this by now.—"Nothing New under the Sun."—That came from King Solomon. Well, maybe UFOs were a new thing, but what about the lines in Cuzco Peru?

If there was nothing new under the sun and this had been going on so many thousand of years, what was going on? Normally when faced with repeated similar situations we should have some kind of mass mental memory or DNA code to read them by. It should be like driving or riding a bike, this exercise of life. Once you know how to do it you always can never forget.

But we could not evolve further from this repeated action. Being Monkey King meant nothing if you could not escape the same constant endless mistakes. He could hear the Kingston Trio singing from the 60s, "When will they ever learn?" in the background..

Same questions generation after generation. No earthly or heavenly movement toward something different that he could possibly see on the horizon. He was just as bad as all those he pointed fingers at. He was convinced everyone on the planet was thinking the same things, just showing it in many different ways.

What a Monkey! He can'tcan't learn anything!

This was the Century of Progress. This Century was great for technology, luxury and the rise of the global standard of living, as well as the independence of so many countries. We were out of the caves. But it was also a great era for genocide, war, starvation and the return of cultural struggle. The Cave was looking pretty good sometimes.

Another night was moving on and still no answers.

The Desert Sun was rising fast. He closed the curtains.

The Monkey was just as perplexed as ever.

Into the Valley of the Ghosts

At some point he had fallen asleep. Not sure when or how. It just came and went. Ah Peng was calling him. It was time to go to the office. Exhausted and starving he woke up to another day in the desert.

After a short while, he was back in the car, heading for his other office over an hour away. This was a trip down memory lane. The apartment was a new thing. He was heading back to where his current roots were in China.

Over 12twelve years ago he had settled in an idyllic small town in China and this is where his office was. He had been there so long he was almost a local. Number Seven hated being here. She preferred the big city life, style and clothes.

This farm town turned Factory City was more his style than hers. With a population of 700seven hundred thousand— ninety-five percent young factory workers—it was busy only on Sundays. He moved there because of the nearby small range of mountains, which in the haze became dreamlike, though in the past four years they were harder and harder to see because of the smog.

When he arrived, there had been no stop lights. Now there were speed cameras and shopping centers. He came here to get away and start a new life and now this life was getting like his old lives, full of regret and mistakes.

But as the Chinese believe in a 12twelve year cycle, so he had become to believe that the cycle had its revolutions and that things would turn again in his favour. This place had taught him so much, meant so much and for all its it shortcomings and his defeats, it was now part of him.

This was one of the thousands of Guangdong boom towns; a boom he had witnessed. Where farms had once stood were rows and rows of factories making anything from shoes to golf clubs to computer monitors. He had watched the town grow day by day. He could remember long walks in a country-side that was now full of roads. It was the kind of growth that, if you were gone for two weeks, you might not recognize this new building or this new place.

It was a constant steady growth as one new factory was completed and another started. They had even begun a ring-road recently. He could not believe the place he had moved to for quiet was now like this. Before, he had to drive 45forty-five minutes to get to an ATM machine. Now the town had fifteen banks and a direct highway to Shenzhen.

The trip that once took 3three hours now took 50fifty minutes. It was a constant culture shock, so much ""improvement"" in such a short time.

But now it was sad. Over thirty percent of the factories were empty. The world economy which his town was established to feed and supply was grinding to a halt. These were tough times for everyone.

He could see the start of the problems and they grew every day. Empty restaurants and shopping centers were the symptoms of this situation. Dreams and Families far away were beginning to suffer. There was nothing clear any more.

The US government bailing out failed banks was the start of a long and profound avalanche that would cripple us all. Thank God #7 had put him on a diet seven weeks ago. It was time to buckle up, and put his shoulder to the millstone. He was privileged or unlucky enough to see the beginning of the great change in our world.

We would be forced to live differently. It was just that simple.

Returning to the office meant back to the struggle. The keyboards were just one problem. He had others. It is funny to see how when it rains it pours.

The office workers were waiting. Not sure what mood he was in. Since he was totally unpredictable, they were never sure. He could be brutal today and the most caring man the next. It was both a failing and his greatest gift. Keep them guessing.

The truth was he did not know himself. Control was not his *forte*, though the Chinese had taught him more about control than anyone else ever could. The Monkey was calculating now. Maybe he was calculating the wrong way, but he was calculating. Maybe he made one bad decision after another, but at least he was thinking; which was a new skill.

Today, he would be silent. He had to think. He went to his upstairs office without saying a word, leaving them in suspense. During the night he had given them the work for the day so really nothing needed to be said.

His office was full of memories. But the memories were not his any more. They were the memories of someone else. He had been humbled by the past several years. As business got tougher, somewhere he had lost his over-confidence. He had changed.

The Monkey was now more human. He could see his own failings as well as the failings of others. He could see that he might not get to the Promised Land. It was really up in the air. After forty years in the desert, it gets a bit depressing. Your best friends turn on you. There is no-one you can trust. False idols look so attractive. He looked around at his books and things with only great regret. He was not the man he thought he was going to be. This office was now just a simple tomb.

He called #7. Of course her phone was off. It was more of the same. Now that she had her money she would be back to the normal routine. The defeat was a rout. Napoleon was defeated. Elba was in sight.

God save the Queen! His heart felt the same old pain. No way out of this.

Thank God, for wireless. He took his computer and went to his room where he could be alone.

Again.

Reviewing his email, he saw more bad news. Two more of his customers were delaying his payments. One had been promising to pay every day for a month and the container was sitting in Mexico. These were not new customers. They were very old customers. The economy was hitting them too. It was sad to see people he had known as young and growing businessmen beginning to renege on commitments. When he had met them they were so hopeful and growing.

Now their customers were not paying them, and they were not paying him. A sure thing was turning to dust. This was affecting him and causing him to pay suppliers late also. It was causing him to think twenty times about everything.

He maliciously thought about the speculators and Goldman Sachs. They had caused all of this by their greed.

They had made money from money that did not exist.

Now the whole world was grinding to a halt. The culprits were fine. The Government was paying their bills and their evil earnings were safe and secure.

Governor Palin, in her hockey-mom suit, was clapping. Senator Obama was shaking his head. Soon they would realize what a mess they were in. He felt sorry for them. They were going to be even more lost than he was.

The wolves and black horsemen were on the far banks of the Hudson and Potomac and the Thames looking for food and very hungry. He could see the mist from their breath and hear the soft snorts of black horses as they pawed the soft ground before our Capitals. They were all smiling.

It was the crime of the century. What a way to start our New Shining Millennium.

What would happen to all of those who could not afford food?

What would happen to the Monkey King?

Caleb Kavon, The Monkey in Me

Since it was morning in China he had to wait until the afternoon to start calling his customers in Europe. He would keep working until late until he had spoken to all his customers.

Another day of trying to get ahead.

This was not exciting or sexy. It is the life of most of us. Another day of labour begins without fantasy. Answering emails, working in fields, cooking meals, delivering things, doing memos, and driving in traffic are the things that consume our short lives on this earth. Some go about this happily. Some go about this with pain. But going about this and that is what we all share. He was no different from anyone and every day he was being cut down to size even more.

Poor Monkey.

Life was not the Da Vinci Code. Stephen King could not answer the questions of life. Tom Clancy could not solve the energy crisis. Harry Potter, oh my God.

Go ahead, Hunt for Red October. It would make no difference. Cancel the Country Club membership before the rioters are back on the street and gunfire can be heard.

Life was eating, breathing and struggling and for him just a little bit of sleep. Until we made that our first priority, nothing was going to change. He knew this was simply not going to convince many, but better tell the truth than live this lie. We had to do something, or we were not even good enough to be Monkeys, much less humans.

After thinking this, he called up all his workers. He gave them each three hundred Renminbi—forty US dollars. He said nothing and then sent them down. He was like this. Good and Bad. But he had a conscience. And it was this conscience which might be his downfall.

How could someone be such a Saint and Total Jerk at the same time?

The Monkey King.

Back to the Computer.

More emails.

A company in Israel wanted to buy one cell-phone. He was going to get rich with this one. Another customer in Australia wanted ninety thousand coffee cups. This might pan out. Hermann'sHermann's assistant had sent the request from Germany, but he wanted a better price. Even a glimpse of light was reassuring somehow.

He had to keep plugging away.

Customers were tough. You love, hate and need them. They determine your very existence.

It was not like being a soldier. There it was kill or be killed. They got you, or you got them. That was nice, especially when they were gone. Yes, there was the ultimate level of stress everyday but it was of a dramatic, high-tension kind. In business, it was a slow burn. You worry everyday, and the worry never goes away. You need to check the email and the bank account.

His problem was also that the customers always thought they could do the same thing he was doing. It did not matter that he had tons of experience and spoke perfect Chinese. They wanted to go and reinvent the wheel. It was few and far between that had real faith in him.

The competition would just not stay dead. This was the most unfortunate part of his new life. The competition kept coming and growing and he was having a tough time keeping up with them.

He was not sorry he had resigned from the military. He was a Cold Warrior. When the Cold Warcold war ended, they wanted him to go to Somalia. He was just not going to shoot starving people. Communist Farmer Guerillas were as far as he would go. If no country could destroy us, why go to Africa, or Bosnia, or prepare for the Blitzkrieg into Iraq?

You fight and swear to defend the Constitution.

He could now see the Spanish Armada leaving the ports.

The Farewell Tour.

Caleb Kavon, The Monkey in Me

We were losing our power by the minute. He was getting sick of listening to the Chinese tell him about the falling dollar.

Of course, they were right. There was nothing in the Constitution about share-holder'sholders' rights but the Government now was bankrupting us forever by letting the bankers off the hook. Shareholder'sShare-holders' rights. Where did that fit into anything?

Life, Liberty and the Pursuit of Happiness was our creed, not the Dow Jones. Remember that.

We were lost.

Let'sLet's pick a fight with Russia. Just what we need:—another Cold War on top of the endless War on Terrorism.

The Dollar was on a Kamikaze Crash Dive. We were jumping off the cliff while the NASCAR season was underway. The Government would run out of money before they cleaned up this mess. It was a fact.

They just did not want it to go down all at once. It was a funny thing. They were going to kill the small investor slowly. We were going to bleed like someone who had slit their wrists in a bathtub—slowly and painfully, a little at a time. Drain them all and let the bankers like Arthur Stein's son survive. The Chinese and the rest of the world were being bled in exactly the same way.

Health Insurance was gone with the Bail-out. Social Security was probably gone too. Pensions were gone. The failure was complete now. There would be no social changes without crisis. They did not know what was going on. We were confused and lost—all together, all of us.

Then he got another call from Australia. The Customers were happy with the samples. Hermann'sHermann's office called with an order and one customer had sent some money. He had some hope. He might survive another month, maybe two.

So it went everyday for the small businessman. There were just little victories and big defeats which were offset by more little victories and more big defeats. You could go from total doom to very hopeful in one minute and back again.

He did believe. It was just hard. He had to keep telling himself he would pull through. He had to stay on the ball. There were no free lunches any more. Wall Street had eaten them all. He had to believe in himself and his strategy. Something would pan out.

He tried #7's phone again. Still turned off.

Feeling satisfied with his business life and miserable as always in his love life, he pursued his day uneventfully until 6pm when he got a call.

This was a rare call. Andy WelshPeter was his oldest comrade in the wilds of China and never called. He had been going through a nasty divorce and had been veering between severe depression and alcoholism for about two years. He had not heard from him for so very long.

AndyPeter was inviting him out to the KTV for the night. He had some business to discuss and would he be ready by 7pm for some fun at the club. Sure, he said.

But this was really weird. AndyPeter was a Scrooge. He never helped pay for anything. If they went to the club, he would not spend a cent.

He got Ah Peng to drive him to the club and invited Austin Joe Li, his good Taiwanese friend. Being with Andy could be Peter was miserable and Austin was good fun. This was a usual event except Andy was never there any more. Maybe tonight would be fun?

Imprints on our Minds VI

In Afghanistan we are fighting Afghanis, Terrorists
and Pakistanis as well as ourselves.
What happens in Las Vegas Stays in Las Vegas, like
some sort of cleansing experience.
Christmas Cards and Calendars
The Royal Asiatic Society in Xian.
 BK Burgers and Taco Bell.
Michael Jackson, we need to follow his life too?.
The Beatles . . . and the Son of Yoko??
High School and Graduation Speeches.
Them and us.
Mandela is great. Mugabe is bad.
Myanmar did nothing.
China did something.
Bangkok is fun.
Mississippi is poor and Bangladesh is a basket-case.
Mississippi still loves McCain.
New Orleans is recovering.
Nuke Iran.
We take care of #1—first, always.
Who is that person, #1? I want to meet him or her.
The Knicks on a Friday.
Paul Newman and Steve McQueen.
Jets and Steelers.
 Jet Blue, what is this?
Slim Fast. Oprah. Tom Cruise.
Putin is KGB. Putin is a UFO?
 Sly Stallone and Meditation, it all fits together.
 Church of Christ and the Mormons.
If we are broke the Chinese will buy it.
Global Warming and the Gold Standard.
Winning on Aggregate.
We can'tcan't believe this is happening to our
portfolio.

Caleb Kavon, The Monkey in Me

Circles in Cornfields.
India is about business?
Winn Dixie .
Enron and Exxon Global and Condaleeza Rice, or
was it Chevron?
Ho Chi Minh .
Elton John.
Ethnic Cleansing and Billy Joel and Joe Biden.
Jim Croce and Alice Cooper without the Golf Course
The Beltway—sounds like some kind of punishment.
Gerald Ford was not smart.
Genesis and the BIBLE
What my Father never told me and the loss of my
Mother.
Nokia and Motorola have market share in Haiti and
DR Congo.
Oklahoma!
Bill Gates changed the world. So did Magic Johnson.
 Red Sox and Cubs. Yankees and Indian
Reservations.
Trump and Ivana, the daughter.
 ""You had no choice.".."
 Norbit.
The Spy who loved me and Marvin Gaye.
Spanish Sahara.
 My First Kiss and the NATO Base in Romania.a
Atlanta is a model of race relations.
Shadow Cabinets and Violence with Knives.s
Many Hues of Blue.
Cubans all hate Castro.
The Pope wins over America.
You should take up golf. It is good for networking.
Mexican politics is messy and Chicago is corrupt.
Brad and the girl from FRIENDS, then 8 children?
Stopping Children from mass violence is not a good
thing.

Caleb Kavon, The Monkey in Me

Cyprus is split in two, so is Korea and that is all we
have now, but we could split Sudan.
Is Sri Lanka split in two? Does Kashmir and the West
Bank count?
Madonna adopting and Getting Divorced. Looks Great
for her Age.
Ellen Degeneris with David Bowie. Let'sLet's Dance!
We know where we are going and the Meaning of
Life.

ParadiseGoodViews

The KTV was a Karaoke Bar. China'sChina's version of Wan Chai.

Here you got a room with a stereo KTV system, and the idea is, you pick a girl to drink and sing with you and maybe take her home. There were all kinds of these, from really basic to really plush. If you had money, this is where you met with friends and the Bosses did business. It was better to do deals here than at the Factories because it was a more friendly environment and conflicts could be discussed in a nice atmosphere.

This particular club was famous. It was opulent and showed all the new wealth in China with. Marble Columns and Rooms decorated in golden trim and big heavy plush sofas. His customers often gasped in admiration when he took them here.

There were 800eight hundred girls who would go in groups from one room to another with a ""Mommy,"", their manager. The girls would make about twenty-five dollars for sitting with you and drinking, and the mommy would make about five dollars per girl. Since a factory worker would make about a hundred and twenty dollars per month, this was good money for all involved.

With the Girls, it was the same story. Poor families and problems at home, and the need for cash led them to this place. They were much younger than the girls in Wan Chai. Normally seventeen to twenty-one years old.

Though prostitution was illegal in China, this was another of those rules not followed and rarely enforced. You did not have to take the girl home with you, though he had taken his fair share over the years.

Going there was both sad and happy. It was here that he had met and begun to fall in love with #6 and #7. Maybe he would meet #8 in the building tonight. But he was still too upset even to consider the possibility..

Caleb Kavon, The Monkey in Me

When you enter the hotel there is a long line of women in fancy long Chinese dresses who shout, ""Good Evening, Welcome to our club.".". And you tell them what room you are going to and one of them escorts you there.

When he got to the room there was AndyPeter with two girls. AndyPeter was about fortyin his early 60s, with a Boston AccentBrooklyn accent, and looked it with his old jeans and checkered blue shirt. He had been the most fun guy in the world about ten years ago. Like himself, he had had a live-in girlfriend and was out every night.

Then he had changed. He became sullen, cynical and critical of everyone. It was probably the divorce. But now he was here having fun again. Maybe there was life after death. If he could recover, anyone could recover.

Andy Peterhad learned to hate Chinese women, calling them greedy. He was a real exile, and had not been in the US for four years. He never went to Shenzhen and like himself lived also only with the Chinese.

AndyPeter was not your normal expat. More of a mountain-man. He would never be able to go back to another life. As much as he seemed to hate it all, you knew he loved it. Despite his miserable exterior he was a real artist and provided tools and hardware gift products to stores all over the US. His Chinese was awful but he was the hardest worker in the world, driving to distant factories every day.

"Andy, what is going on? You said you had had enough of this life?"

"Well Bobby, tonight, I just want to get drunk. My divorce is now final. Where is your girlfriend?"

"She'sShe's gone and I might as well forget it all, Andy.Peter. Really upset every day. It's seven weeks now."

"What'sWhat's your problem, Bobby? Just forget her. It means nothing. Take another one tonight, screw her and forget about your greedy girlfriend. She is just using you for your money. You know that, don'tdon't you?"

"I thought this was different. You are probably right, but it hurts. I really loved this one."

"Talk about me, Bobby! Look at you. Mr Ten girlfriends and now you are moping like this every day. You should have learned your lesson after the last one. You broke up with her and were depressed again. You'reYou're looking for romance and there is none to find here. It's almost ridiculous to see you like this. No Love here, just a struggle for security. Wake Up!"

"Yes, drink up! I forgot to bring the absinthe."

"You are such a jerk, Bobby. I was hoping you would bring some."

With that, girls started coming in. Six or 7seven at a time. There were all types. Tall. Short. And there were so many. They just kept coming in. You could pick as many as you wanted, but had to pay them each twenty-five dollars. All the Managers knew him, some for over ten years. It was always like a homecoming when he was at the club. After he was with #7, he had not been there very much.

He called #7 again. The phone was still off. He had been fooled.

In the room, there was what was called a DJ—a girl to pour the drinks and change the songs on the Karaoke machine—and a waiter who would bring in the booze and other things. You had to pay them tips too and pay for the room. If you were lucky, the night would cost two hundred dollars and usually more. Some of the big Bosses could spend two thousand dollars a night.

Entertaining was a big thing in China. It was a way to show off your wealth and influence people, and this was the way to do it. Boss WangWu was famous for his parties. The Three Tigers hated to go out.

After seeing about fifty girls, he picked two. One was absolutely beautiful, with black hair and a movie-star face. The other was plain, with very large breasts. The beautiful one was smiling at him with black eyes that shimmered like diamonds. What a pick!

""There you go, Bobby. Forget the last one. She was nothing. She fooled you. I knew this would happen. You are just too nice to them. They see a sucker like you, and just rip you off. There was nothing there. You really should know better."

"Great, AndyPeter! I know you are happy about the divorce, but you were a bigger mess than me for the past couple of years. I am glad that you are coming out of your shell."

"I sure am. Look at me now. Have another drink." ."

Soon AustinJoe Li came in. He was Taiwanese with big round glasses and a cell-phone on his belt and one his oldest friends. He was another story of resilience. Born fifty years ago to an impoverished family in Taiwan, he had managed to get an education and became quite rich with a factory in China.

Then about ten years ago, Austin had lost everything in a bad deal with a mainland politician. He had been beaten severely by hired thugs and thrown in jail. He was in hospital for seven weeks with his cheek-bone crushed and eye-socket damaged. He visited him in hospital and remembered his wife crying by the bedside. It took months to recover.—Crazy things happen in China. AustinJoe had suffered some of the worst.

Anyone else would have left forever, but not Austin.Joe. He carried on and started a new business. He was just always hopeful and smiling. They had become instant friends ever since. He was the kind of guy that made Taiwan famous, and one of the great factory managers that began the boom here in China.

AustinJoe was always going to be trying to get ahead and never was going to hang his head low. He was having bad times again and drinking too much, but at least they were with friends. He was the most friendly guy in China. With all the problems he had suffered, he never became bitter. His luck was bad but he believed it would change and maybe it would. He could speak some English.

""Bottoms up, Andy!Peter! Bottoms Up, Everyone! Enjoy tonight!

"Thanks, AustinJoe. Look at Bobby! He is so sad."

"Yes, AndyPeter. Bobby is too romantic. But, 'Bottoms Up!' Bobby."

"Thanks, AndyJoe. 'Bottoms up'!.""

And so the night went. They talked a bit about business and drank a lot. They were three lost souls in the desert. The beautiful girl was smiling at his Chinese jokes all night. She liked him and was stunning. He was alternately angry at #7 and happy with the new girl. He got her number. AndyPeter took one of his girls in the bathroom to check out the merchandise. AustinJoe started dancing and was really wasted. The night flew by.

It was justJust another night in China while the world was falling.

Another day of wandering in the Desert was ending. They were all talking about the Golden Calf. Moses was nowhere in sight. He was still alone.

Heavy drinking and young women are a good team. This is what they did to relax. It would not bring #7 back to him but it was better than the pain he had been suffering. The new girl looked like just maybe she would not be a misery. She was nice, soft-spoken and not aggressive. She asked him why he looked so lonely and sad.

Maybe.

Besides she was stunning beyond words and had just arrived from a very far-away province. She said she hated working at the club and wanted just a nice quiet life. She liked him a lot. Could he call her tomorrow?

Maybe.

AndyPeter was happy too. He was divorced and could relax. Strange, he liked one of his girls too. This was the first time in about three years. He had suffered for three years and now was happy for the first time. AustinJoe was very drunk and dancing, inviting everyone to drink.

The Roman God of Wine was blessing this night. Everyone was happy. The girls were smiling and playful. This was a nice night. Even better, his customer from Guatemala called and said he had a new order. This was turning out to be a great day.

He might survive again. Thank God for Austin.Joe. Thank God for Andy.Peter. He might survive all of this. The pain was leaving him. This was the best night in seven weeks. There was hope again.

Maybe they would be able to leave this desert. He sobered up. It was all in the hands of God. The Land of Milk and Honey was not yet even near. But the stars through the window were lovely and just maybe one day they could cross over.

Ah Peng came to pick him up at 1am. He got back to his room and began to think.

Norwalk Wisconsin 1968

The #7 thing was getting to him again. Soon it would be eight weeks of this. He was angry.

He called her again. The phone was off.

Would this ever end?

A cool, blue anger.

As if he wanted her to come back somehow and beg him to be at his side. As if something bad would happen and she would repent. As if he would be the one to have to forgive her from his great loving heart. It was just a desire for some sort of revenge. Love was dying.

If she did not know herself at all, how could she love him?

How could you love someone you never knew?

He thought back to his youth. One day in 1968, he was driving through the Wisconsin country side, near a place called Norwalk.

His parents had just had a nasty loud fight. He hadn'thadn't seen it, but it could be heard from his room. The end was near. They would soon divorce, never to see each other again.

His father then took him and his brother on a drive. His Father loved just driving along for hours without any real destination. Kmart had just opened in Altoona Wisconsin, and he mentioned it to his Father.

His Father said there was no way they were going to Kmart, when it was so beautiful and peaceful here in the country side of Norwalk, and asked why would he want to go there? Did we know that he had been to Norwalk Connecticut? And he thought there was also a Norwalk in Ohio and one in California too. So many towns named Norwalk in the US, wasn'twasn't that something?

He could remember the tall silos and the cornfields of the late Wisconsin fall and the country roads winding and rising and falling. It was a grey-cloudy day and they just drove in silence.

His Father was obviously sad and hardly said another thing for the rest of the day. The silence was only overcome by the occasional noise of the sedan'ssedan's tires on some gravel that had entered the road from a nearby farm driveway, or a small rush of cold wind that came in from the window, slightly opened when he was smoking one of his Camel cigarettes, with one hand on the black steering wheel.

This is what he wanted with #7. He wanted her to be no more than this; just a passing memory like this one of his dead father on the afternoon of a long distant day. He wanted her to be no more real than this memory of yellow-brown cornfields and sombre corn silos. Or no more real than the presence of his now dead Father, who had left this earth, and was just another person that he had never known.

If she could somehow just pass to this place; he could deal with it. She could be just a thought that passes before our eyes when we are ready to sleep, and is just as easily sent back to the depths from where it came.

She could become just this, a thought whose feeling was gone long ago. In the end, everything goes to this place including #7 and all that she ever was, as his Father had gone there before her.

If only she could go there today, all would be better. And yes, she was well on the way. To kill a Ghost, you need to call them Ghosts. She was going there with his Father.

At his Father'sFather's funeral ten years ago, they lowered the casket and everyone left as if running away. He stayed to watch the undertaker remove the canopy and finally put all the dirt on the grave.

It was only the right thing to do. This running away was cowardly. He had to live the funeral to its very end. Alone with the undertaker and the wet reddish dirt hitting the casket on a brilliant fall day, he could live and die through it all. It could pass into memory.

Today he was beginning to throw dirt on the grave of this love. Number Seven was being buried and he would see it through until the dirt was level and the grass could grow. Then he could let the Sun shine again in his world.

That was all he could do.

It was over.

Go Ahead andLarry King could play the Air Guitarair guitar to your heart's content.

The Monkey could see it all.

Finally.

We would all slide down together.

What was done was done.

The Call of the Promised Land was getting louder. The Angels were singing, and that sound was sweet and true.calling.

The desert could be beautiful sometimes, especially in the hours before the arrival of another day and the harsh reality of the sun.

Oh God He missed her.

He fell asleep.

The End

CHINA, HONG KONG & South-East ASIA FICTION
PUBLISHED BY PROVERSE

Andy Carter. Bright Lights and White Nights. 2015.

Peter Gregoire. Article 109. 2012.
    (Winner of the Proverse Prize 2011.)

Peter Gregoire. The Devil You Know. 2014.

Lawrence Gray. Cop Show Heaven. 2015.

Dragoş Ilca. HK Hollow. 2017.

Caleb Kavon. The Monkey in Me. 2009.

Caleb Kavon. The Reluctant Terrorist.2011.

Caleb Kavon. Paranoia. 2012.

Ivy Ngeow. Cry of the Flying Rhino. 2017.
    (Winner of the Proverse Prize 2016.)

Jan Pearson. Black Tortoise Winter. 2016.

Jan Pearson. Red Bird Summer. 2014.

Jan Pearson. Tiger Autumn. 2015.

Jason S Polley. Cemetery Miss You. 2011.

James Tam. Man's Last Song. 2013.

Paul Ting. Bao Bao's Odyssey: From Mao's Shanghai to Capitalist Hong Kong.

CHINA, HONG KONG & MACAU NON-FICTION
PUBLISHED BY PROVERSE

Jean A. Berlie. The Chinese of Macau: A Decade after the Handover. 2012.

Gillian Bickley, Ed. The Complete Court Cases of Magistrate Frederick Stewart. 2008.

Gillian Bickley. Ed. The Development of Education in Hong Kong, 1841-1898 as Revealed by the Early Education Reports of the Hong Kong Government 1848-1896. 2002.

Gillian Bickley. The Golden Needle: The Biography of Frederick Stewart (1836-1889). 1997.

Gillian Bickley, Verner Bickley, Christopher Coghlan, Timothy Hamlett, Geoffrey Roper, Gary Tallentire. Ed Gillian Bickley. A Magistrate's Court in Nineteenth Century Hong Kong. 1st ed. 2005, 2nd ed. 2009.

Major (Ret'd) Brian Finch, MCIL. A Faithful Record of the *Lisbon Maru* Incident. 2017. Translation from Chinese with additional material. 2017.

George Washington (Farley) Heard. Through American Eyes: The Journals (18 May 1859 - 1 September 1860) Of George Washington (Farley) Heard (1837-1875). Edited by Gillian Bickley. 2017.

Sophronia Liu. A Shimmering Sea: Hong Kong Stories (Winner of the Proverse Prize 2012). 2013.

James McCarthy. The Diplomat of Kashgar: A Very Special Agent. The Life of Sir George Macartney, 18 January 1867 to 19 May 1945. (Winner of the Proverse Prize 2013). 2014.

Stuart McDouall. All Agog In China. 2014.

Lt. Cmdr. Henry C.S. Collingwood-Selby, R.N. (1898-1992). Richard Collingwood-Selby (Chile) and Gillian Bickley (Hong Kong), Eds. In Time of War. 2013.

FIND OUT MORE ABOUT PROVERSE AUTHORS, TITLES, EVENTS AND LITERARY PRIZES

Visit our website: http://www.proversepublishing.com

Visit our distributor's website: <www.chineseupress.com>

Follow us on Twitter
Follow news and conversation: twitter.com/Proversebooks>
OR
Copy and paste the following to your browser window and
follow the instructions: https://twitter.com/#!/ProverseBooks

"Like" us on www.facebook.com/ProversePress

Request our free E-Newsletter
Send your request to info@proversepublishing.com.

Availability
Most titles are available in Hong Kong and world-wide
from our Hong Kong based Distributor, The Chinese University
of Hong Kong Press, The Chinese University of Hong Kong,
Shatin, NT, Hong Kong SAR, China.
Email: cup-bus@cuhk.edu.hk
Website: <www.chineseupress.com>.

All titles are available from Proverse Hong Kong,
http://www.proversepublishing.com
and the Proverse Hong Kong UK-based Distributor.

Stock-holding retailers
Hong Kong (Growhouse, Bookazine)
Singapore (Select Books),
Canada (Elizabeth Campbell Books),
Andorra (Llibreria La Puça, La Llibreria).
Orders from bookshops in the UK and elsewhere.

Ebooks
Many of our titles are available also as Ebooks.

www.ingramcontent.com/pod-product-compliance
Lightning Source LLC
Chambersburg PA
CBHW050348030726
47503CB00008B/2669